"Mommy!" R
echoed along

Hayden gripped his Glock and held it low, his finger down the side of the barrel. It was likely Ruthie had simply had a nightmare.

But given all that had happened, he wasn't taking any chances.

The alarm blared, adding to the cacophony of sound both outside and inside of Hayden. Either his fellow investigators had rushed in to help or someone was trying to escape.

"Mommy!" Ruthie screamed again. Her bedroom door flew open, and a tiny rocket dressed in *PAW Patrol* pajamas streaked past him. She threw herself into her mother's arms, sobbing.

At least she was safe.

Mia gathered the shaking little girl to her chest and whispered soothing sounds that had no actual words in them, just comfort.

Now wasn't the time for them to huddle in the hallway in the open. While it might have been a nightmare, there could also be an active threat...

Jodie Bailey writes novels about freedom and the heroes who fight for it. Her novel *Crossfire* won a 2015 RT Reviewers' Choice Best Book Award. She is convinced a camping trip to the beach with her family, a good cup of coffee and a great book can cure all ills. Jodie lives in North Carolina with her husband, her daughter and two dogs.

Visit the Author Profile page at LoveInspired.com for more titles.

Taken at Christmas

JODIE BAILEY

LOVE INSPIRED SUSPENSE
INSPIRATIONAL ROMANCE

LOVE INSPIRED SUSPENSE
INSPIRATIONAL ROMANCE

PLEASE RECYCLE · THIS PRODUCT IS RECYCLABLE

Recycling programs
for this product may
not exist in your area.

ISBN-13: 978-1-335-98029-8

Taken at Christmas

Copyright © 2024 by Jodie Bailey

Love Inspired
22 Adelaide St. West, 41st Floor
Toronto, Ontario M5H 4E3, Canada
www.LoveInspired.com

Printed in Lithuania

MIX
Paper | Supporting
responsible forestry
FSC® C021394

Thine eyes did see my substance, yet being unperfect; and in thy book all my members were written, which in continuance were fashioned, when as yet there was none of them.
—*Psalm* 139:16

To Kay King

You once told me I could be anything I wanted to be...

And I believed you.

Thank you.

ONE

Why is that woman carrying a backpack?

Mia Galloway set aside her phone, which displayed the Are you okay? text she'd typed to her daughter's birth mother, Paige Crosby, and tried to breathe normally. The conversations in the crowded café seemed to soak into the dark wood walls, retreating into a dull roar as Mia's anxiety rose. The fact that Paige had asked to meet and was now nearly half an hour late only heightened her tension.

The woman, in her late twenties with a small scar on her temple and tousled blond hair that made it appear she'd just crawled out of bed, wound slowly between the tables, her gaze darting nervously. Something about her was familiar, but the full memory wouldn't form.

What was in the blue backpack held over her shoulder in a white-knuckled grip? Why was she so skittish? Mia's stint in the army had taught her that out-of-place backpacks and nervous strangers meant danger.

And after she became a deputy, a dark November night, lit by flashing red and blue lights, had taught her that not even the home front was safe.

The woman stopped in the center of the room, one hand nervously tapping the backpack's strap.

She was up to no good.

Mia's heart pounded. Sweat sheened her skin. Dark dots swam in her vision. She should sound the alarm before something terrible happened. If she didn't—

The woman's blue eyes locked on to Mia's and narrowed. After a silent stare down, she seemed to almost smile, then turned and darted out, disappearing into the lobby.

Mia gripped the sides of her chair. Had that woman been looking for her? For Paige? Where had she gone?

Outside the plate glass windows that fronted Harvest Café, shoppers strode along the riverwalk, arms laden with bags as they enjoyed the sights and sounds of Christmas in the historic town. The unusually cold weather hadn't kept revelers from clogging Wincombe's downtown.

There was no sign of the woman.

Around her, other diners chatted and laughed as the longing strains of "I'll Be Home for Christmas" drifted down from the speakers. They behaved as though nothing bad could happen here.

But it could.

Mia dug her fingers into the wooden chair. That song brought to mind movies that featured scenes of a soldier fighting a horrific battle intercut with images of a family celebrating joyfully around a tree, smiling unaware as their loved one died a terrible death.

She shuddered. There had been Christmas music pouring through the speakers of the Double R Convenience Store on that November night when—

Shaking off the memory, Mia scanned the room, her emotions screaming for flight while her mind reasoned that it would be foolish to rush out of the restaurant when she had no idea if the danger was real.

She couldn't stay here, though. There were too many people. Too much noise. Too many colors.

Hands shaking, Mia pocketed her phone, tossed a twenty onto the table and bolted for the door, desperate for fresh air. She'd text Paige to meet her at home. What had her daughter's birth mother been thinking when she suggested they meet downtown on the busiest tourist day of the year? She knew how Mia reacted to crowds.

"Ma'am? Are you—"

Mia ignored the hostess's concern and burst onto the sidewalk, letting the door slam behind her as she looked left and right for a place void of the Christmas crowd.

There. An empty bench on the riverwalk offered an oasis amid the people clogging River Street, which had been closed for the upcoming Christmas parade. Hurling herself across the uneven cobblestones, Mia dropped onto the bench and braced her hands on her knees, gulping damp December air until the vise around her chest eased and her thoughts settled.

Shame chased the panic, searing her skin and heart with an entirely different sort of burn.

She was a grown woman. A mother. A former soldier and deputy sheriff. And yet…

She ran from shadows and fled nonexistent threats. That woman had probably reacted to Mia's frightened stare, nothing more.

Turning her face to the sky, she dug her thumbs into her knees. *Come on, God. It doesn't have to be this way. You could make this better. You could take away this fear.*

There was only silence.

Mia sat back and drew another deep breath, desperate not to call attention to herself. Her display in the café had done a fine job of that already. The last thing she needed was for law enforcement to respond to a call about a woman falling apart in the middle of the Christmas cheer.

The festive music and decorations had her emotions spun

up more than usual. That was all. She'd known better than to come to River Street on the Saturday before Christmas. Tourists flocked to the small town of Wincombe on the Inner Banks of North Carolina to shop on the historic streets that reflected the town's colonial village roots, to watch the street parade in the morning and the boat parade on the river after dark. The normally quiet town was nearly burst with people celebrating the season.

She'd hesitated to meet in town, but Paige had been insistent about getting together as soon as possible in a public place and without Ruthie. It was an odd request. Her daughter's birth mother had never been shy about coming by the house, even spending weekends with Ruthie and Mia on occasion. Mia considered Paige to be like a sister, but today Paige had seemed hesitant to speak and had refused an invitation to the house.

Then she'd been a no-show. Mia's concern had already been heightened by Paige's unanswered calls and unread texts when she'd spotted the woman with the backpack. It was a perfect storm of panic, given that Paige was thirty minutes late and the café had grown more crowded as lunchtime neared.

Inhaling another fortifying breath, Mia pulled her cell from her pocket and flicked the screen, sending the Are you okay? text she'd already typed.

Like the four before it, the message went unread.

This wasn't like Paige. A student at East Carolina University, Paige was conscientious and kind, driven to succeed but compassionate at the same time. She would make an amazing social worker after she graduated with her master's degree in the spring, and Mia would be her biggest cheerleader. After all, she owed Paige for one of the greatest gifts in her life.

When Paige had learned she was pregnant as a college

freshman, she'd reached out to Mia and her husband, Keith, at their small church, where they had been requesting prayer during their infertility journey. Paige had been bold in asking if they wanted to adopt her unborn child and, after weeks of prayer, they'd agreed.

Although adoption hadn't been on their original agenda, it had turned out to be the exact right plan. Ruthie was now a perfect little four-year-old girl.

But becoming a widow four months after Ruthie's birth hadn't been something Mia had ever imagined.

She'd also never imagined PTSD so severe that it would rip away her career as a Tyrrell County sheriff's deputy.

Mia shuddered and reflexively flicked her finger over the screen to call Paige. Four rings then voicemail. Where was she?

Adrenaline waning, Mia tapped her finger against the screen, calling the one person who would listen to her fears without judgment.

Hayden McGrath answered on the first ring. "What's up?"

Relaxing into the sound of his familiar voice, Mia stared across the Scuppernong River toward where it emptied into the Albemarle Sound. "Paige hasn't shown, and I nearly accused a woman of being a suicide bomber. I'm having a fabulous day. How's my daughter?"

Hayden was Ruthie's godfather and Mia's closest friend. He had been beside her the night her world shattered. He'd been Keith's best friend and her colleague. Hayden and his now former fiancée, Beth, had walked Mia through her darkest days.

"Your daughter conned me out of half of the books in the kids' section at Booker's, then managed to wrangle ice cream out of me at Tastee Cone."

The lighthearted rundown of her daughter's morning

eased Mia's tension. "It's barely lunchtime, and she's having cake at Ashley's birthday party later. If she's sick half the night, I'm calling you."

"She's a kid. She'll be fine. I've pumped her up with more sugar than that when you weren't looking."

"You did what?"

Hayden continued like she hadn't spoken. "And she keeps reciting her line for the Christmas play over and over again."

Mia chuckled. "Yeah, she's excited." That was the understatement of the year. The play tomorrow night could not come quickly enough.

"I just dropped her off at Javi's for Ashley's party, and I'm actually headed your way to see if I can find some lunch. What are your plans since Paige hasn't shown?"

"Not going back into Harvest Café, that's for sure." Everyone would eye her with pity or suspicion. She ran her finger along the seam of her jeans. Now that she was in fresh air, the whole incident seemed silly. "I just want out of the crowds." She'd have to head directly through them to get to a quieter, safer place, so she really couldn't win.

"Hey, no putting yourself down. You've been through a lot. From a literal war zone when you were in the army to… Well, it's been a lot, and you're doing great." A stretch of silence let road noise filter through his truck's Bluetooth. "As for Paige, maybe she slept in. Want me to drive by her parents' house and see if she's there? She's home for winter break, right?"

Mia twisted her lip and stood, turning to scan faces as she leaned against the metal railing about ten feet above the river. "Maybe she put her phone on silent and she's just running late. It's nuts down here." The crowd was getting thicker, and it spilled from the street onto the riverwalk. A man's shoulder brushed hers as he passed. Turning toward the river in an effort to ignore the growing mass of humanity, Mia stared into the water, trying to ignore the people clogging the sidewalk. "Don't check up on her like she's a child." Another shopper bumped her back, shoving her against the rail.

"I understand. Hey, when Ruthie and I were in Booker's, I saw their special in the café today is a French dip, your favorite. You're only a couple of blocks away, and they weren't busy. The crowds seem to be concentrated on River Street. Why don't you text Paige that you're headed there, then we can grab a bite while you wait for her. I'll meet you at the end of Watchman's Alley."

Smart. The narrow alley curved between two buildings and was covered by an arched brick roof. It would be quiet, as most people chose the wider sidewalks along Water Street to get to the riverfront.

Mia dashed across the cobblestone street, and her shoulders relaxed as she stepped into the quiet alley. "Hang on." She pulled the phone from her ear, grateful that Hayden understood the PTSD that shadowed her life. Her thumbs tapped the screen. Heading over to Book—

Footsteps pounded into the alley behind her, echoing off the ceiling.

Before she could turn, a force shoved into her back, driving her to the brick floor. Her phone flew from her fingers and skittered along the ground. A palm pressed against her head, grinding her cheek against the gritty bricks.

Mia tried to scream, but the oxygen had been driven from her lungs. Her muscles seized. She couldn't move. Couldn't breathe. Couldn't fight. Reality vanished, and all she could see was Keith in a pool of blood, ripped violently from her life.

Now she was the victim. It was her worst nightmare.

Fight. Fight for Ruthie. Her mind screamed. Her body

refused to respond. She had to do something. She couldn't leave her daughter as an orphan. She couldn't—

The weight shifted, and hot breath hit her ear with a deep hiss. "Your daughter deserves better than you."

"Mia?" Hayden McGrath's voice pitched up, echoing off the arched brick roof of Watchman's Alley. What had happened?

He dashed into the dim space and rounded the bend, his heart racing to a frantic beat.

A figure in baggy jeans and an oversize purple East Carolina hoodie pinned Mia face down, a brick raised to smash into her skull.

Hayden's feet stumbled on the uneven brick. "Stop!"

At Hayden's shout, Mia's assailant jerked back. The person pulled the brick higher over their head, increasing the chances a blow would be fatal. Sunglasses covered their eyes. A mask obscured the lower half of their face.

With her attacker off balance, Mia clearly saw a chance to save herself. As Hayden ran closer, Mia bucked, throwing her attacker to the side.

The brick flew, bouncing off the wall before it clattered to the ground.

The person rolled, scrambled up and raced toward River Street.

As Mia leaped to her feet, Hayden dashed past, bursting into the cold sunlight at the end of the alley. He looked left and right along the crowded street.

The mass of people was too thick to spot his target. Multiple tourists sported the iconic purple of East Carolina University, which was only an hour away. No one seemed to be disturbed and nothing seemed out of place, so Mia's attacker had probably slowed when entering the crowd, lowering their hoodie in order to blend in.

Hayden's shoulders slumped. There was nothing he could do. Sure, he would have Mia file a report, open an investigation and wait for the sheriff's department to pull camera footage from the businesses closest to Watchman's Alley, but that would take time.

But in the moment, he'd failed.

"He got away?" Mia appeared beside him, eyeing the crowds she'd been so frantic to escape only moments before. Little had either of them known the multitudes she'd feared had offered her protection.

When Hayden faced her, he winced. A dark red mark marred her cheek, small scratches from the grit on the brick leaving thin red streaks in what would likely be a bruise by morning. He let his hand hover near her face. "Are you hurt?"

Mia jerked back. Her breaths sped up, and she backed into the alley, her eyes on Hayden. "I'm fine. I'm—" But her head swung back and forth as though her body wouldn't allow her to continue the lie.

She was definitely not *fine*. Not when she'd just lived through something very close to both of their worst nightmares.

As though her knees refused to hold her anymore, Mia sank onto a bench halfway up the alley and bent forward, her elbows on her knees. "What just… How did… Hayden?"

He hadn't heard that kind of desperate, helpless plea in her voice since the night Keith was murdered.

There was no way they were going to find her assailant today, and Mia needed him more than he needed to rush into the street to search for witnesses. He went to her, praying no one else would venture into the alley, and knelt in front of her. Resting his hands on top of hers, he bent to look into her eyes.

The fear in her expression nearly undid him.

"Mia, I am so sorry I wasn't here sooner." He should have told her to stay by the river until he reached her. He should have suggested she keep to the crowds instead of venturing into the deserted alley. He should have—

"No." Mia sniffed and raised her head, trying to put on a brave front although her fingers shook beneath his palms. Her skin was so pale that the red bruise and scratches seemed to glow in the semidarkness. "Not your fault." The words trembled. She swallowed hard and sat taller. "I'll be fine."

He knew better than to let her retreat into herself. Over the past four years, she'd become the queen of stuffing things inside to deal with at a later time that never seemed to come. It was the coping mechanism she used to hold panic attacks at bay. Since Keith's murder, she'd lived in a state of extreme fear and mild paranoia. She knew every route to every exit, and she lived in the small spaces that she could control. Crowds were her kryptonite.

Mia also played the guilt game like a champion. Hayden did as well. They'd both been on duty the night the call had come about an armed robbery in progress at the Double R Convenience Store on Highway 64. They'd both responded. If either of them had arrived even one minute earlier, then Keith might be alive today.

Fear and guilt had been unleashed on that night, and they hovered over Mia's life as well as his own.

But this wasn't paranoia. It was real, and Mia needed to face reality if she wanted to get through this, no matter how hard it was.

"Mia, I let you fall into the hands of an opportunist who was waiting for—"

"No." Mia's face collapsed. As if someone had thrown her into a deep freeze, she trembled from head to toe. "No. I messed up. I—" The words rattled and quaked.

Hayden was on the bench beside her in an instant. He wrapped his arms around her and pulled her close to his side. She shuddered as though someone had grabbed her shoulders and was shaking them.

He'd walked her through a panic attack before, but this one felt different.

No, this wasn't a panic attack. When she was in the throes of fear, Mia didn't want to be touched. She preferred to be left alone while she fought the darkness until she regained control. Right now, she seemed to seek safety as she clung to him.

Mia breathed in through her nose and out through her mouth, trying to center herself. The breaths were stuttered, but at least she wasn't hyperventilating.

Hayden waited, his grip on her shoulder tightening. Someone had hurt her, and he wanted to race out into the street to search for the perpetrator and mete out justice. To ask them why anyone would want to take down a seemingly defenseless woman who had already been through more than enough in her lifetime.

With a deep breath that caught in her throat, Mia shook her head. "I froze. I froze and then—"

"It's understandable." He couldn't let her condemn herself over her reaction to a traumatic event, one that was doubly horrible for someone whose life had already been shredded by horrific violence.

"No." Mia jerked free and rocketed to her feet. She whirled on Hayden. "I froze. I couldn't protect myself, not even for Ruthie." Her words echoed off the bricks. "I kept thinking I had to. She could have been an orphan, Hayden. She could have…have lost me today and…" Her eyes widened, and she stepped back as though someone had pushed her. Her face paled as her hands flew to her mouth. "Hayden."

"What?" He stood and reached for her as she swayed, grabbing her upper arms to steady her. "You remembered something."

"That person said…" She lowered her hands, her gaze locked on to his. "Said my daughter deserves better than me."

Hayden's own knees reacted to her words. For a second, it was tough to tell if he was holding Mia up or if she was supporting him. "This was targeted."

"By someone who knows me. Or at least knows about me." She lifted her gaze to the arched brick ceiling. "I have to get to Ruthie." She pulled away from Hayden. "If someone came after me, they might make a run at her, and I can't… If I lose…"

There was nothing more to say. Hayden was right there with her. He'd protect his goddaughter with his life.

Reaching for Mia's hand, he tugged her into a run toward his truck, which was in the parking lot at Booker's. "I'll drive." They made it to the truck and buckled up in record time. He looked both ways before pulling onto Fifth Street. "Call Javi." Ashley's father, who was throwing the birthday party Ruthie was attending, was a deputy who'd worked with both of them. He'd protect Ruthie until they arrived. "Tell him what's happened but caution him to be careful not to alarm the kids. Let him know that no one is to pick Ruthie up except us, no matter who they are or what they say." Javi was a good father and friend who would handle this with care and discretion. "Have him contact the sheriff as well." Everything had happened so fast that he hadn't even considered calling law enforcement. Someone needed to retrieve that brick in case it held evidence that could lead to Mia's attacker.

With trembling fingers and words, Mia made the call, then rested her phone on her knee. "Hay?"

He didn't take his eyes off the road. The uncertainty in her voice spoke the question without her having to ask it out loud. "I don't know if Paige is involved in this, but I hope not." On their run for the truck, the horrible thought had formed. Paige had been a no-show for a lunch with Mia that she'd requested. She was the reason Mia had been downtown.

"She knows I don't do crowds, but she asked to meet me on River Street. I mean—"

"But the woman in the café. How would she know about that? It seems like she might have been a random person."

"But what if she wasn't? What if someone sent her to spook me so I'd run? If someone knows me, they'd know what would push me over the edge. They'd get me to flee, and they'd know I'd take a path out of the crowd. All they'd have to do is follow me."

It seemed like a big risk that depended on a lot of uncontrollable variables. Unless she was right and someone had been watching the whole time, just waiting for a chance. Still… "What would the motive be? Why would Paige set up something like this? You guys have had a great relationship since long before Ruthie was born. She approached you about adopting. She's practically your sister. If she was feeling some kind of way, she'd have told you."

"Maybe." Her voice was uncertain as she dragged her thumb down the side of her phone. "But if it wasn't Paige, then where is she?"

He wished he knew the answer to that question, because either Paige was behind the attack or she was also in danger.

TWO

For a small town, Wincombe suddenly seemed very large.

Mia wrapped her fingers under her thighs and dug into her jeans. The handful of miles to Javi's house felt like a cross-country road trip. While Hayden pushed the speed limit, he didn't roar over it. The streets were too narrow and often filled with people walking or pushing children in strollers, even during this unusual cold snap.

Still, he could go a little faster. Leaning toward the windshield of Hayden's blue pickup made her feel like she was closer to Ruthie, even though that was foolishness.

"Hey." Hayden's voice was irritatingly calm. "Everything will be fine. Javi won't let anything happen to Ruthie, and I won't let anything happen to you."

It was a nice thought, but Mia didn't relax. She wouldn't be at ease until she had her little girl in her arms.

Maybe not even then.

"So..." The tone in Hayden's voice was familiar. He was shifting into investigator mode. He'd left the sheriff's department not long after she'd stepped away, bruised by Keith's murder but not broken as she had been. For the past three years, he'd been living an hour away in Elizabeth City, working for Trinity Investigations. The organization worked closely with attorneys and other law enforcement agencies to reinvestigate complicated cases from the beginning, ensuring that no evidence of guilt or innocence had been overlooked before trial. Occasionally, they assisted during complicated investigations, offering additional eyes and minds.

She looked over at Hayden, whose white knuckles betrayed his anxiety. Talking often kept him mentally focused and out of his emotions, so she might as well humor him. Conversation might help her as well. "Ask whatever is on your mind."

He navigated a turn off of Highway 64 onto Raleigh Street, headed toward the river through an older neighborhood. "Can you talk about what happened in the alley? Get the details out before they fade?"

The last thing she wanted to do was relive those awful moments, but he was right. The more she spoke while the memories were fresh, the more she'd be able to offer investigators later. Mia closed her eyes, trying to envision every detail. She walked Hayden through the moments leading up to the attack, forcing herself to look at the scene through an emotionless lens. If she allowed the terror of the moment to invade, it would overwhelm her and shut down her system. "Whoever it was had me pinned. He..." Her hand went to her cheek, the sting at her light touch indicating that a bruise was forming. "Well, you saw. You came in right after he took me to the ground."

"And he said...?" The words were gentle, but steel wound through them. Hayden was angry, but was it at the perpetrator? Or was he upset that he hadn't arrived sooner? He viewed himself as her protector as well as Ruthie's, and he stumbled under the weight of guilt when he believed he'd fallen short.

"It's not your fault." She tried to force the truth across the space between them. He carried so much guilt from the night

Keith died. They'd both responded to the call, not realizing that the armed robbery in progress was about to change their lives. Hayden had been the first on the scene, and Mia had pulled into the parking lot less than a minute behind him. All of the reports said Keith was dead before they arrived, but she'd lain awake too many nights wondering what would have happened if she'd driven faster.

How often had she heard Hayden say the same about himself? She couldn't let him carry the burden of today's attack as well.

Hayden spoke before she could. "I asked what the guy said, not who's at fault."

Mia winced at the sharp retort, then bit the tip of her tongue. Neither of them needed to spiral into their emotions. They were raw from the events of the day and from the events of four years ago. "Like I told you, he said, 'Your daughter deserves better than you.'" Her stomach shuddered despite her best efforts to maintain emotional distance. *Why?* Because of the PTSD? Because of the sleepless nights she paced the house? Because she tended to shelter her daughter instead of letting her explore the world around her? Because—

"Mia, listen. No matter what some lowlife says, you're the most amazing mom I know. Don't beat yourself up over some creep's threat." He slowed and turned onto Columbia Drive. "We keep saying *he*. Are you certain it was a man?"

"It wasn't Paige." There was no way. Despite their earlier suspicions, everything about the attack went against Paige's nature.

"I didn't say it was, but I couldn't tell if it was a man or a woman. The oversize sweatshirt, the baggy jeans, the hood, the mask, the sunglasses… Everything happened so fast, it was impossible to tell anything unique about the person. You were the closest, and you keep saying it was a male. I just want you to be sure when you talk to the sheriff."

No matter how hard she tried to remember, there was no way to say for certain. "Given that assaults like this are typically perpetrated by men, I assume it was a male. The words were hissed, so I couldn't describe their voice. They were solid. They were strong, but I can't say with certainty. I can only tell you what my gut says."

As they pulled into Javi's driveway, Hayden scanned the area, searching for threats Mia didn't want to consider. "Go inside and see Ruthie. I'll call Sheriff Davidson and arrange for him to meet us at your house to take your statement." Wincombe was too small for a dedicated police department and relied on the sheriff for law enforcement.

"Okay." As soon as Hayden stopped behind Javi's Bronco, Mia turned for the door.

Hayden's hand on her shoulder stopped her. "I know that I'm not a parent and that you're Ruthie's mom, but you're understandably spun up right now." His grip tightened, though it remained gentle. "Don't frighten her by drowning her with your fear."

If anyone else said such a thing, she'd rage in anger, but Hayden was right. Ruthie had no idea what her mother had endured, either today or on the night her father died. She was simply a four-year-old enjoying a friend's birthday party. The last thing she needed was for her mother to snatch her away from the fun. At her age, being hastily pulled out of a much-anticipated party would be a major event.

Mia needed to slow down and settle for watching her daughter play with the other kids if she wanted to maintain Ruthie's innocence.

She took a deep breath and squared her shoulders. No matter how much she wanted to rush in and pull her child close, she was the mommy. Her daughter would take cues from her. With great effort, Mia shoved her emotions into the dark place where they couldn't touch her and locked them away.

It was the opposite of what her therapist told her to do. Cramming away the emotions made her numb and took her out of the moment, but it was the only way she could get through this without subjecting Ruthie to the trauma of watching her mother fall to pieces.

When she got out of the car, Hayden was already calling the sheriff. They'd find the person who did this to her, and hopefully the ordeal would be over by nightfall.

As soon as Mia's shoes hit the sidewalk, Javi stepped onto the porch, shutting the door behind him. At just over six feet and a regular at the gym, Javi was an intimidating force when he was in uniform. Given that she'd been friends with him and his wife, Celia, for years, he looked more like a big ol' teddy bear to her, especially now, when he was wearing a very ugly Grinch Christmas sweater.

It was almost enough to make her smile.

Javi caught her expression and looked down at his chest. "Yeah, we'll do anything to make our kids laugh, right? Ashley picked this thing out and wanted me to wear it for her fifth birthday." The amusement in his dark eyes disappeared as quickly as it flared. "Ruthie is fine. They're in the den watching Jim Carrey do his Grinch thing since it was too cold for them to play outside. You want to talk about what's going on or go in and see her?"

That was code for *Are you going to freak out the kids, or do you need a minute to pull yourself together?*

"I'm fine. I know Ruthie is safe, and it's enough to be close to her." It would be a different story tonight, when she tried to sleep. The terror would rush in once her house was dark.

But that was a problem for later. "Hayden is with me. He's on the phone with Sheriff Davidson." She gave Javi a quick, bare-facts rundown of the situation.

Javi crossed his arms over his chest, nodding soberly. "I don't blame you for rushing over here. I'd want to get to my kid quick if someone said something like that to me. And no sign of Paige?"

Paige had been a fixture at church and had volunteered often with the children's department. Everyone knew her well, particularly the parents. "I don't think—"

Javi held up his hand. "I didn't say she was involved, but I'm concerned about her. She covered the nursery when Ashley was a baby and worked in the toddler class on Sundays when she was older. Paige is a solid kid. I'm more concerned about—"

"Someone coming after her, too?" It was chilling that Javi's thoughts ran along the same tracks as her own. With Paige not answering her phone and someone directly attacking Mia as a parent, it made sense that Ruthie's birth mother might be in the crosshairs as well, although motive was a sticky question. "I'm not sure what's happening, but—"

A slamming truck door stopped her. "Mia. Javi." Hayden's tone was urgent. Gravel crunched under his feet as he jogged up the driveway. He stopped beside Mia, angling so he could see both her and Javi at the same time.

Something dark furrowed his brow. He wasn't the type to overreact, so whatever the sheriff had said must be bad.

Mia grabbed his elbow. "Is it Paige?"

"Deputy Angeles called the house and talked to her mother. Paige left over an hour ago to meet you." He flicked a glance at Javi, carrying on an unspoken conversation.

"What are you not saying?" Mia's grip on Hayden's elbow tightened. "I'm a big girl, Hay. I used to be a deputy, too, in case you forgot. Don't treat me like a child just because I'm going through some things."

"Some things?" Hayden clamped his mouth shut, seeming to realize the terse comment might have gone too far. "I'm sorry." He pulled his elbow from her grasp and stepped closer as though she might need support. "Deputy Angeles traced the route from her house to River Street, and when he got into town…" He exhaled loudly.

Mia's ears roared. She'd seen Hayden's expression before, and it only came when he was delivering bad news. "What?"

"Angeles found Paige's car in the lot at the end of River Street. There are signs of a struggle. Her phone and purse are in the back seat. Mia, I'm sorry. It looks like Paige may have been kidnapped."

"I'm really not sure what's happening, Elliott, but I don't think I need you to send in some kind of geared-up quasi SWAT team." Pressing the phone tighter to his ear, Hayden stepped farther into Mia's backyard, away from the stairs that led to the covered wooden deck. Although Mia was inside the house, the last thing he needed was for her to come outside and overhear this conversation with his boss. They'd come here to await the sheriff after letting Ruthie enjoy the remainder of the party.

He walked farther onto the wide lawn that ran to the river. Although the water view was obscured by a privacy fence, the soft sound of the Scuppernong making its lazy way to the Albemarle Sound whispered in his ears.

Normally, the melody of the water was relaxing, but not today. After all that had happened over the past few hours, it only served to grate his nerves.

Over the phone, Elliott Weiss, founder of Trinity Investigations, chuckled. Somehow, every time he did that, it sounded slightly sarcastic. The former Special Forces soldier carried a healthy dose of cynicism, and it bled into most of his interactions so that even his humor seemed laced with it. Still, he was a good boss and a better friend, one of the few people in the world whom Hayden trusted completely.

"Nothing's funny, man." Hayden wasn't in the mood for humor or sarcasm.

"So the comment that implied I was going to go full battle rattle and come fast-roping out of a Chinook onto the roof of Mia's house wasn't supposed to be funny?"

"Not really. It was more of a—"

"Warning?" Elliott's deep voice held a thin thread of amusement. "I get it, McGrath. We all know I can be a little too full-steam-ahead sometimes. I freely admit it." His tone turned serious. "You can tell me what's going on, but I reserve any promises about how I'll respond until the end."

It was tough to tell if Elliott would be hands-off, but Hayden needed to talk to someone who wasn't involved. He'd never get his head cleared otherwise.

Walking to the fence, he flicked the padlock on the gate, then leaned against the wood slats, facing the house so that he would see Mia if she stepped outside. She was already keyed up waiting for someone to come and take her statement about the attack. She refused to stop cleaning the downstairs while Ruthie napped.

Overhearing the full details surrounding Paige's disappearance would only make things worse.

Hayden ran down a quick summary of the attack on Mia and their race to Javi's. After a peek at Ruthie so she could see for herself that her daughter was safe, Mia had stayed at the party while Hayden went to speak with Sheriff Davidson and Deputy Angeles, whom he'd worked with in the sheriff's department. What they'd told him and what he'd seen…

He dragged his hand down his face, wishing he could erase the images.

"So you're certain this thing with Mia was targeted?" A soft scratching in the background indicated that Elliott had pulled his trademark yellow legal pad from his desk drawer and was making notes with a sharpened number two pencil. The man might only be in his late thirties, but he was old-school through and through.

"It had to be. Mia was alone, yet her attacker specifically mentioned her daughter. If nothing else, they've seen the two of them together before. Whoever it was, they would have cracked her skull open with that brick if I hadn't gotten there when I did. That seems personal." Hayden leaned forward, trying to relieve the slight nausea that plagued him. He'd been too late to save Keith, and he'd nearly been too late to save Mia, but he couldn't think about that now. There was too much at stake to risk losing focus. "It gets a lot worse."

"Go on." Elliott was still writing.

Hayden waited for him to finish, hunching his shoulders against a stiff breeze that blew between the fence slats. He should have grabbed his coat. "I left Mia at Javi's and was on-site at a distance while they processed Paige's car." He almost wished he'd stayed away. "It's not just that they found her phone and her purse. There was blood. Lots of blood." Almost as much as the night Keith had been shot.

Elliott's sigh was heavy. "Too much?"

"Hard to tell. I wasn't allowed to get too close, and you know how a little can look like a lot, but… It was enough to concern me. Obviously, we won't know whose blood it is until lab results come back, but the facts point to it being Paige's. If it is, she may not have survived whatever happened to her."

"Let's operate on the assumption that it's hers. Given what

we know, that's the most likely scenario. Was it in the passenger's seat or driver's seat?"

"Passenger's."

"So if it's Paige's blood, she wasn't driving the car."

"No. And here's what I don't understand… How did someone get to her when she was parked in the lot at the end of River Street? How did no one see anything? The lot was swarming with people. If someone wanted to hurt her or take her, they'd have done it somewhere secluded. Her house is surrounded by trees and set back from the road. She drives up an isolated strip of two-lane road with woods on both sides in order to get to downtown."

"You're too close to this. Take a step back and get your emotions out of the way."

When Hayden had resigned from the sheriff's department after Keith's murder, questioning his abilities and instincts, he'd reached out to a buddy from his army days, seeking guidance. Elliott had just started Trinity Investigations, and he'd been happy to bring an old friend into the fold. He'd funded Hayden's training as an investigator, putting him through classes and working with him on cases. Technically, Hayden was the junior investigator on the team of seven, and Elliott was always working on ways to hone their skills.

Hayden exhaled and closed his eyes. He tried to treat the scene as though he'd seen it in a textbook, as though it was a puzzle to be solved, not as the place where Ruthie's birth mother had likely been in danger…or worse.

He'd been standing about twenty feet away, so the details were fuzzy, but it wasn't always the details that mattered. The important thing to look at here was the actions of the criminal.

He replayed his conversation with one of the deputies, who'd pointed out that the area where the car was parked was beneath a tree in a blind spot to the cameras at either end of the lot. While there might be a shot of the car pulling into the lot, it was likely the cameras wouldn't have been able to pick up the car after it parked.

A shot of the car pulling in...

Hayden's eyes flew open. "Paige probably wasn't attacked in the parking lot. She was probably never even near it. She was attacked somewhere else, then someone moved her car because they wanted to throw us off."

"Those are my thoughts as well." The background was silent. Elliott had stopped writing.

Hayden could practically see him studying his notes. While the man had been a more than capable SF operator, his mind had always been one that noticed details and put together puzzles. "There's another angle to consider. It's possible that Paige's disappearance isn't about her at all. It's possible it's meant to serve as a threat to Mia or Ruthie."

"But why?" Hayden slumped against the fence. "Wait a second..." Was this more about Ruthie than Mia? "Ruthie's birth father is a guy named Blake Darby. He and Paige dated for several years, and he fully supported the adoption, but what if he's having second thoughts?" Bile nearly gagged him. "What if he wants to take her for himself?"

"I'd say that's a stretch if he's never expressed regret, but it's not out of the realm of possibility. I'm sure he's already on the sheriff's radar, given that he was the boyfriend. He's the first one they'll look at in Paige's disappearance, even though he has no history of violence. I will say it's a good thing you're in town, though. Sounds to me like Ruthie and Mia are going to need you now more than they ever have." Elliott cleared his throat. "Speaking of that...have you told Mia why you're really there?"

"Not yet. I told her I came home early for Christmas." Although he'd received his assignment several weeks ago, every time he'd tried to tell Mia about it, the words had choked him. He'd arrived at his parents' house the night before and had told Mia he'd take Ruthie for the morning so she could meet Paige, but he'd said little else. "I was planning to sit down with her after I brought Ruthie back home this afternoon, but now…" He dragged his hand across his face, his palm scrubbing against stubble. "It might be too much for her to hear right now."

"Time won't make it easier."

The sound of tires crunching gravel pulled Hayden's attention toward the front of the house, where the lights atop a sheriff's department SUV were just visible over the front privacy fence. He should go inside to give his statement and to support Mia as she gave hers.

Then he'd have to find a way to tell her that Trinity Investigations had sent him to Wincombe on an assignment that might just tilt her world and catapult them both straight into darkness.

THREE

Mia shut the door behind Sheriff Davidson as he left and leaned her forehead against the cool painted steel. She'd rehashed the morning so many times that the telling had become rote. Far from being overwrought, she was drained. Between the attack and Paige's disappearance, her emotional capacity was drained. She couldn't *feel* any more.

She was simply exhausted. Although it was only five in the evening, she was ready for bed.

Except she wasn't. Once she shut off the lights and pulled the blankets to her chin later this evening, the day's images would hunt her in the darkness, chased by wild conjectures of what might be happening to Paige. The night hours would drag on for sleepless years.

Footsteps rushed in thuds across the hardwood entry, and tiny arms wrapped around her thighs. "Mommy!"

Despite everything, Mia smiled. Lately, she heard *Mommy* shouted more than spoken. She leaned down to pull her daughter's head against her stomach and wrapped her arms around precious little shoulders. No matter how tumultuous life was, she needed to paste on a brave face for her daughter.

"Ruthie!" Mia yelled in return, then planted a kiss on Ruthie's sandy-blond hair. "How about you find your inside voice and drag it out from wherever it's hiding?"

Ruthie giggled and whispered loudly, "Is this better?"

"Very nice. Now, what do you need?"

Wriggling away, Ruthie planted her hands on her hips and looked up with a very serious expression. "Can we have hamburgers for dinner?"

Mia mimicked her posture. "Is that a Ruthie request or an Uncle Hayden request?" Left to her own devices, Ruthie would eat fish sticks with mac and cheese for every meal, every day. Hayden, on the other hand, referred to himself as a "meat-atarian." All red meat, all the time.

Ruthie's head tilted, and she pursed her lips. It was a look that said *Do I tell the truth or do I make up a wild story?*

That child had a tell that gave her away every time. Mia smiled. "The truth, little ma'am."

Ruthie wrinkled her nose. "An Uncle Hayden request, but he said he'd make them on the stove like Noni does."

"Well, since he wants to do the cooking, how can I refuse?" If he was going to fry burgers like her grandmother did, then she was all in. Noni soaked bread in milk, chopped up onions, then mixed it all together with ground beef. She fried the patties until crispy edges—

Her mouth watered at the thought of her favorite comfort food, and she smiled at the thought of Noni, who'd arrive on Christmas Eve. Although her parents were out of town on a Christmas cruise, they'd celebrate quietly with her grandmother.

"Yay!" Clapping her hands, Ruthie bounced on her tiptoes, then bolted up the hallway into the kitchen, screaming Hayden's name.

Mia shook her head. Anyone would think the idea had been Ruthie's. That girl would do just about anything for "Uncle Hayden." Since he'd moved to Elizabeth City to work for Trinity, they saw him less often, which meant his visits were more of a reason for Ruthie to get spun up.

Having Hayden in town for a few days allowed Mia to breathe easier, even after the drama of her morning and her concern for Paige. Hayden staying close by at his mom's house on Eighth Street always tended to make her feel a little more secure.

That was a phenomenon she didn't want to read too much into.

After double-checking that she'd turned the dead bolt, Mia wandered through the house, closing the plantation blinds. Detouring through the living room, she plugged in the Christmas tree, and the white lights glowed against the soft white walls, dark hardwoods and denim-blue furniture.

If she had her way, she'd avoid decorating for the holiday, but Ruthie deserved to celebrate like other little girls who hadn't violently lost their fathers two days after Thanksgiving. So for a few weeks a year, she managed to grin and bear it as her refuge became a reminder.

After Keith's murder, PTSD had driven Mia inside with uncontrolled agoraphobia. She had taken out her excess emotions on the remodel she and Keith had planned but had never found time to complete. She'd worked with her father to polish the dark hardwoods. They'd painted the walls a cheerful white, and she'd scoured the internet for deals on decor that gave the home an airy waterfront vibe.

When a colony of bees had settled behind the siding, she'd opted to have the entire exterior of the house redone as well. While it had been a circumstance she hadn't foreseen and an interesting journey, it had afforded her the opportunity to create a "new" home from her "old" one. It was truly her safe space.

Although she was now able to venture out, life was anything but "normal." She maintained careful control, knew all of the exits and was always on edge, waiting for the next panic attack to stop her in her tracks. Her home remained the one place she felt truly safe.

Keith's life insurance had provided enough to care for herself and Ruthie, but she ached to work again, to move forward into the detective position she'd always longed for.

Given the certainty of diving into violent crimes like the one that had stolen her husband, a return to her career was impossible. She envied Hayden's job, although he sometimes dealt with cases she'd never be able to handle.

When she made her way to the kitchen, Hayden was alone at the large island. He looked at home amid the dark hardwoods and white cabinets. He looked kind of handsome in his green Henley.

Not that she'd ever tell him that.

Mia slid onto the bench in the U-shaped breakfast nook by the bay window, where Hayden had already closed the blinds. "Where's Ruthie?"

He looked up from slicing an onion. "Upstairs. She stole my phone and started a video call with Noni." As assortment of veggies from her fridge were scattered across the deep blue granite counter. "Apparently, she doesn't trust that I know what I'm doing in the kitchen and needs confirmation. Also, that kid works my phone better than I do. It's embarrassing."

"Which is weird, because I never let her play with my phone. Could it be that somebody else in this kitchen has handed theirs over too many times when the chattering from the back seat got out of control?"

Hayden scanned the ceiling with exaggerated innocence, then looked at her. "I called my mom. She's running by the store to pick up the stuff for burgers and bringing my things over from her house. I'm bunking on your couch tonight. You and Ruthie shouldn't be alone."

Mia didn't protest. As much as she wanted to argue that she could take care of herself, there was no denying that danger lurked closer than she cared to admit. She and Ruthie would be safer with Hayden here. She'd also sleep better with him in shouting distance.

It wouldn't be the first time he'd camped on her couch. It had happened so often when he lived in town that she'd purposely bought an extra-deep sofa so he could be relatively comfortable.

Mia fingered the fringe of a blue-and-white-striped place mat. Hayden was a better friend than she deserved. He certainly sacrificed more for her and Ruthie than she could ever repay.

Hayden cleared his throat. "I need to talk to you about something."

The shift in his tone lifted her head. Was he finally going to tell her everything he'd learned about Paige's disappearance? It was obvious he was holding back details.

Hayden slid the onions onto the plate, then grabbed a tomato, intently creating perfectly even slices. "There's a reason I'm in town, and it's not because of Christmas."

Mia's fingers froze, his words not remotely close to what she'd expected. Given that the multiple shocks of the day had shorted out her ability to react, his tone pooled dread in her stomach rather than inciting panic. Was something wrong with his parents? With him?

What would happen if she lost her closest friend? She wasn't sure she could survive another bout with grief.

Hayden glanced up, then returned his focus to the tomato. "Trinity caught an assignment from the State Bureau of Investigation. The SBI is putting together a case against an organized crime ring, and they want an outside party to re-investigate a handful of crimes that may be tied to the ring."

She wasn't sure where he was headed with this conversation. Hayden had worked several investigations for Trinity, looking back through cases as though they were brand-new so that law enforcement or attorneys could be certain no details had been missed. There was no need for him to be so concerned, unless—

Her hand went to her mouth. "Keith." Her late husband's name breathed between her fingers.

Laying the knife aside, Hayden braced his hands wide on the counter. "The SBI has tied together a string of armed robberies and have linked them to a drug ring. They aren't certain if the robbery on the night of Keith's death is connected. Since it's unsolved, they want everything looked at again to see if they're onto something or if they're tilting at windmills. Since I was on scene that night, Elliott asked if I could take point."

Curling her lips between her teeth, Mia stared at the shuttered windows. Though she'd thought her feelings were squashed by the overwhelming stress of the day, the pain that washed over her was sharp, drawing tears. "So they might finally know who killed him?"

Hayden was quiet so long, she looked over at him. He hadn't moved, but he watched her intently. "I can't comment on an investigation other than to tell you that it's happening."

After four years, there might be a lead in the shooting death of her husband. Numb, Mia slipped off the bench and mechanically made her way upstairs, pausing outside Ruthie's door.

Her daughter chattered away to her great-grandmother, who lived on the other side of the state in Flat Rock.

The pain ebbed and flowed, a sickening cycle of grief

and numbness as suffering tried to break through her spent emotions.

She shut the door to her room and sank to the chair in the corner. Bracing her elbows on her knees, she buried her face in her hands.

Downstairs, the doorbell rang.

She ignored it. Hayden would let his mother in. She wasn't up to polite conversation.

Hayden's words had unlocked the memories she typically held at bay. On the night Keith was murdered, Hayden had just come on duty and she had been about to call it a night. Thanks to a rash of holiday-partying-impaired drivers, she'd worked overtime.

Keith had left the house around eleven to pick up the diapers she should have brought home. He'd assured her he was fine, but mom guilt was real. She'd only been back on shift for a couple of weeks after taking time off for Ruthie's birth, and it had been tough being away.

When the call came about a silent alarm at the Double R Convenience Store on Highway 64, she'd sped toward the scene and had arrived right after Hayden. The store had gas pumps and entrances on two sides, with the cash register situated in the center of the convenience store. Through the front windows, a masked gunman paced in front of the cashier, waving a pistol, his shouts muffled by the glass.

They'd thought no one else was in the store until Hayden had moved to the street side of the building while Mia circled around to the second entry on the back side, keeping to the shadows at the edges of the lot.

She'd frozen when she saw Keith's Ford Explorer parked near the second entrance.

On the other side of the glass door, her husband lay near

the register, blood pooling beneath him and Ruthie's baby carrier beside him.

She had few memories past that point.

Hayden had found her on her knees, frozen in shock, after backup roared onto the scene.

The shooter had disappeared on foot.

Mia rocketed to her feet, fighting nausea. She hadn't rushed forward to help her husband or her baby. She hadn't been strong enough to rescue them.

No, she'd collapsed.

And because she'd failed, Keith's killer had escaped.

Her husband was dead...

Because of her.

After a relatively quiet dinner and an evening fueled by Ruthie's emotional overload, the house was finally quiet. Hayden opened the wide plantation blinds that covered the French doors. The living room was lit only by a soft night-light that glowed through the arched opening to the kitchen, so the night outside was clearly visible. With the house elevated nearly one story to protect from potential river flooding, he could see the moonlight sparkling on the river, though the low bank was obscured by the privacy fence.

He skirted the coffee table and dropped onto the sofa that faced the doors. Sitting back against the cushions, he stared out at the water and the stars above it. He was avoiding his closed laptop, which rested in the center of the square white barnwood coffee table.

At least with the blinds open, the house didn't feel so much like a walled-off prison.

In fact, with the inside lights off, the moonlight outside shone brighter, revealing a night that was clear and calm and beautiful.

If only the home's interior had been that peaceful.

Ruthie had been so keyed up after dinner that it had taken Mia over an hour to get her ready for bed. It was likely the little girl had picked up on the tension in the adults without being able to articulate what she was feeling. For nearly an hour, she'd repeatedly shouted her lines for the upcoming church Christmas play, insisting they listen. When Mia put her in time-out, she continued to recite. After a splashing bath that Hayden had cleaned up while Mia handled her daughter's screaming hissy fit, Ruthie had finally dropped off sometime after ten.

About fifteen minutes ago, shortly before one, the floors in Mia's room had stopped creaking. The sounds from above his head said she'd paced for a long time before settling. Hopefully, she'd fallen asleep, though he wasn't sure how likely that was. Today had been horrific for her, starting with the attack and Paige's disappearance, then ending with his news about a possible lead on Keith's killer.

He should have waited to drop that bomb, but he felt guilty keeping it from her. She deserved to know he would be digging into the night that had derailed her life and had shifted his onto an entirely different track.

Dragging his hands down his face, Hayden stared into the night.

Although search teams were out in force, there was no news about Paige. Javi had texted shortly after midnight to pass along what little he'd learned. A team had spent the afternoon investigating the two-lane back road that Paige had traveled from her house, as it was the likeliest scene of an attack, but there was no intel yet.

Cameras near the downtown parking lot had picked up Paige's car entering with only a driver, but glare prevented them from seeing details through the windshield. Only the steering wheel had been clear, and the person wore gloves. They'd idled at a partial blind spot in the lot until a space opened under the trees where the camera's view was obstructed. After that, they'd apparently slipped away through backyards and alongside streets, because they were never caught on camera again. The sheriff's department was seeking doorbell camera videos from along the street, though they weren't hopeful. Clearly, whoever had ditched the car knew enough to avoid video detection, so they were familiar with the area or had studied it beforehand. This wasn't a random attack. Someone had clearly targeted Paige and possibly Mia.

All of the evidence indicated that Paige's attacker had parked the car and vanished about ten minutes before Mia's assault. That was plenty of time to make it to the alley.

Hayden stretched his neck, mentally walking the route from the parking lot to Watchman's Alley. There were a lot of moving pieces that had to fall into place just right for this to be the work of a single perpetrator. Additionally, he couldn't conceive of a clear motive for a coordinated attack on Mia and Paige. The only connecting link was Ruthie, but no one had come after his goddaughter while she was in his care or Javi's.

Nothing made sense.

Dropping his head to the back of the couch, Hayden stared at the dark ceiling. *Lord, please bring Paige back to her family safely. We need some sort of clue. Something to lead us to where Paige is and to who's behind this.*

He curled his lip. Yeah, that was a familiar prayer. He'd prayed for information so many times over the past four years. He'd argued with God again and again over why Mia and Ruthie had lost Keith, especially so soon after the adoption was finalized.

Maybe investigating Keith's death for Trinity was the answer to that prayer. The county had done a thorough investigation and had come to a dead end, but perhaps fresh eyes would yield something worthwhile.

If he could do this.

Sitting up, Hayden slid to the edge of the couch and pulled his laptop closer, resting his fingers on the top of the case. The files it contained seemed to burn his skin. He hadn't expected the text from Elliott that had come during dinner. The one that said the state had sent security camera footage from the night of the murder.

Footage Hayden had never watched. The pain of losing his best friend had been too sharp.

He'd grown up with Keith Galloway. They'd played together in the nursery at Riverside Christian Church from the moment they were old enough to walk. They'd gone to school together from pre-K all the way to high school graduation. They'd been the closest of friends and had remained tight even when Hayden joined the military and Keith went to ECU to get his degree in cybersecurity.

While Hayden had spent six years defending the country against the physical worst that her enemies could attack with, Keith had spent those same years defending against the technological worst that her enemies could devise. He'd taken a job with the state of North Carolina, working remotely from home and occasionally traveling to monitor network infrastructure for the Department of Transportation.

Keith and Mia had dated since middle school, parting ways only when he left for college. Mia had been two years younger than Hayden and Keith, though she'd returned from her four years in the military around the same time as Hayden returned from his six. Although Keith and Mia had been apart for several years, they'd picked up where they'd left off, marrying within months of their reunion. Still long-ing to serve, she'd joined Hayden as a deputy in the Tyrrell County Sheriff's Department.

Maybe if he'd kept his mouth shut about how much he loved being a deputy and how good it might be for her…

Hayden jerked his hands from the computer, then stood and walked to the door. *No.* Those were mental paths he couldn't wander. If Mia hadn't been on duty, then *she* might have been the one on a late-night diaper run when the rob-bery went down. Or Keith could have died another way. Or any number of a thousand possibilities.

So many verses in the Bible said that God knew what was going to happen in their lives from before they were born. If he believed that was true, then why did he lie awake at night wrestling with why horrible things happened?

With a heavy sigh, Hayden turned his back on the night beyond the glass and stared at his laptop in the near dark-ness. He'd volunteered to take point on this investigation, needing to see justice for Keith. Needing to find closure. Needing to atone for his failures.

He hadn't considered the emotional toll diving into the past would take on him. While he should have known he'd be given access to the video that documented Keith's final moments, the thought hadn't crossed his mind until Elliott's message dinged into his inbox.

Crossing to the couch, Hayden eased onto the cushion, opened the laptop and keyed in his password. He logged on through a virtual private network, then navigated to his work email and opened Elliott's last message. Sliding the pointer to the video attachment, he let his finger hover over the track pad.

This was what it felt like to teeter on the brink. Once he watched the footage, he'd never be able to unsee it.

He pulled his hand into his lap. That night already dripped evil over his nightmares. Once he pressed Play, the horror of Keith lying face down in his own blood would cease to be a static image. He'd have the sound of the gunshot and the motion of Keith's last breath seared into his brain.

He should call Elliott and tell him he couldn't do this. With immediate danger closing in on the two people he cared most about in the world and with Paige missing, this storm was already bigger than he could handle. He should take a leave of absence and help Mia deal with what was swirling around her in the present.

He should not open an emotional can of worms from the past. They might turn out to be poisonous snakes that could devour all of them.

But nobody else at Trinity had firsthand knowledge of that night. If he wanted to bring Keith's killer to justice and bring closure to Mia and to himself, then he needed to set his emotions aside and face the past.

Tilting his head, he listened to be sure Mia wasn't roaming the house. The last thing either of them needed was her walking into the living room to the sights and sounds of her husband's murder.

With a silent garbled prayer for his stomach to endure what he was about to view, Hayden clicked on the attachment.

The video played automatically though silently. He couldn't bring himself to turn up the laptop's volume. He needed to absorb the scene one sense at a time. He'd play it for as long as he could, then stop until he was ready to start again. The first time through would be the worst.

Hayden leaned forward, elbows braced on his knees and

fingers clasped so tightly they ached. His body tensed as the gunman entered the store, his sweatshirt hood pulled over his head and a blue medical mask covering the lower half of his face.

The cashier behind the counter tensed, watching intently as the man wandered the aisles.

What was the gunman waiting for?

Hayden's eyebrows drew together. Was he trying to gather his courage? Waiting for a signal from someone outside? Most armed robbers got in and out as quickly as possible. This guy was either an amateur or he had an agenda.

Given the fact that this case might be linked to organized crime, the "amateur" angle likely wouldn't pan out.

But why was this guy wandering the aisles?

Headlights swept the windows near the side of the convenience store, capturing the cashier's attention.

Hayden's hand shot forward and smacked the space bar, pausing the scene. His breaths came rapidly. His palms dampened with sweat. His heart pounded.

Keith was about to walk into the store holding baby Ruthie's carrier.

He had reached the last moments of his best friend's life, captured forever on video.

Hayden closed his eyes. Maybe he couldn't do this. Maybe—

A distant thump sounded from the backyard.

Hayden jumped up as the laptop screen timed out and went dark. He walked around the coffee table to the door as he strained to hear over the sound of his own heartbeat. Maybe he'd imagined it. Maybe Mia or Ruthie had gotten out of bed. Maybe—

A shadow moved near the rear gate in the privacy fence,

eerie and shapeless in the blue moonlight. Something on their clothing caught the light, then went dark.

Someone was in the yard…

And they were headed for the house.

FOUR

The shadow moved slowly and deliberately, keeping close to the tall wooden privacy fence. The person appeared to be carrying something heavy in one hand, leaning with the weight of their burden.

This was a foe and not a friend, and they'd worked hard to gain entry to Mia's backyard. Mia kept heavy-duty padlocks on the front and rear gates of the privacy fence. There was no way someone had managed to unlock the fence from the outside, so that noise he'd heard had probably been an intruder scaling the fence or removing slats in order to slip through.

He clenched his fists and eased closer to the door, keeping to the side to watch the figure's slow approach. A flash of light occasionally bounced off the person's shirt and pants. *Odd.* Anyone sneaking in should want to be invisible, not... reflective? They almost seemed to be wearing the kind of reflective tape that runners used in order to be seen at night. Why?

Hayden forced himself to focus on the bigger problem. He had no way to defend himself. His investigative position with Trinity didn't require carrying a firearm. Although he kept one locked away at his house, he hadn't imagined he'd need to bring it to Wincombe to defend Mia and Ruthie.

All he had was training and the element of surprise. Combatives in the army had taught him some hand-to-hand techniques, but he was definitely rusty.

Hopefully it would be enough.

If he went out the French doors, he risked immediate confrontation, because he'd be visible from the trespasser's position. His only option was the door that led out of the kitchen onto the side deck. If he could slip out quietly, he could stay low as he circled the deck, using the railing to partially camouflage his movements. That should allow him to make it down the stairs to ground level without being spotted.

If he revealed his presence, he lost his only advantage.

With a prayer for safety, he padded across the hardwood in his socks and grabbed his phone from the coffee table. In the kitchen, he texted Javi to come quickly and to run silent. It was quicker to reach out to a buddy on duty than to deal with the emergency call center and dispatch.

Pocketing the phone, he made his way to the door. He should probably wait for help to arrive, but if he hesitated, the fight might make its way into the house. While he should probably alert Mia, he didn't want to pull his attention from the intruder, and he didn't want to traumatize her if he didn't have to. Hopefully, he could handle this and have the bad guy hauled away with minimal fanfare.

Grabbing the spare key off the counter as he passed, Hayden stopped in front of the alarm keypad. Entering the code would cause the keypad to chime. Hopefully, it wouldn't alert Mia. He held his breath as he beeped through the code, then hesitated.

No sound came from above.

Exhaling, he grabbed the key from the drawer and slipped it into the lock. The click of the dead bolt sounded like a gunshot in the silent kitchen, though it was unlikely the sound traveled. He pocketed the key and eased onto the porch, locking the door behind him. Crouching below the level of the deck railing, he crept along until he made his way to the rear of the house.

After several breathless moments, he spotted a quick flash of light in an open space near the house. The intruder had left the shelter of the fence and was making his way quickly across the open side yard. Likely, they were heading for the porch stairs.

They'd be surprised when they realized Mia had installed a shoulder-high locked gate at the foot of the stairs.

As the figure disappeared from view, Hayden moved to the top step and pressed his back to the wall, waiting for the person below to rattle the locked gate.

Silence.

Where was he? Hayden eased down a few steps, listening. There was only a slight rustle near the gate, barely audible in the cold, silent night.

Were they trying to access the garage under the house? Would they scale the fence and try to circle around to enter through the front door? That would be foolish, putting them in view of the street. What was the—

A sloshing sound rose from ground level. Within seconds, a familiar, horrifying odor wafted past.

Gasoline.

Hayden pressed tighter against the wall about halfway down the steps, his heart racing. This guy wasn't trying to come inside.

He was attempting to smoke them out.

If he set fire to the house, it would force Mia and Ruthie out. They'd run outside in a panic without a plan, making them easy targets.

There was no way Hayden would let that happen. This house was Mia's safe place. Not only was it his responsibility to protect her and Ruthie, it was also his duty to protect the one place where she felt secure.

No longer caring if he was heard, Hayden raced down the wooden steps, his footfalls clattering against the wood. He hit the gate at the bottom hard, then stopped to listen. The sloshing had stopped, but he had no idea where the person had gone.

There wasn't time to figure it out.

Flipping the dead bolt, Hayden shoved the heavy wooden gate with all of his strength.

The door collided with something hard.

A muffled grunt and a curse told Hayden he'd struck a blow. He stepped around the door to find a person scrambling to their feet.

Balling his fists, he addressed the figure, who wore what appeared to be baggy pants and a bulky coat. "Get up. Now." Javi would be here soon. All he had to do was keep this guy from lighting a match or getting away.

This ended now.

The person paused, head bent. Rising slowly, they moved their hands to their neck, pulling something up over the lower half of their face. Based on the person's broad-shouldered bulk and stance, he was dealing with a man.

Moonlight glittered off reflective strips on the person's jacket and at his ankles.

Was he wearing…? Hayden squinted. Was he wearing turnout gear?

Sure enough, when the guy came to his feet, hands out to the sides, the dim light revealed the heavy baggy pants and bulky jacket of a firefighter.

What was happening here?

The two men squared off. Although the other guy had a

couple of inches of height advantage, Hayden wasn't worried. The heavy gear would hamper his opponent in a fight.

The man flexed his fists.

"I wouldn't if I were you." Hayden pulled himself to his full height. "The sheriff is already on the way. This is over."

"Not by a long shot." The man growled and lunged at Hayden, driving him backward against one of the thick posts that lofted the porch one story off the ground.

Hayden's head cracked against the heavy wood, and he stumbled forward, shaking his head to get his bearings while stars whirled in his vision.

It was enough to give his attacker the advantage. The man shoved Hayden in the chest, pushing him backward into the plastic trash cans beside the house, the clatter deafening. As Hayden scrambled in the heap of bins, the man ran for the back gate.

Hayden stumbled to his feet and gave chase, but the guy had too much of a head start.

He squeezed through the space where two slats had been removed. Just as Hayden reached the fence, the sound of a small engine reached his ears.

Hayden staggered out onto a narrow river beach, his socks sinking in damp dirt. A small fishing boat with an outboard motor roared across the river, headed for the other side.

Hayden balled his fists and fought the urge to punch the privacy fence. An injured hand wouldn't help Mia. It wouldn't bring that guy back. It wouldn't end this war.

His shoulders slumped with the weight of failure. By the time the sheriff's department got boats on the water, that guy would be long gone.

Hayden trudged toward the house, trying to shake off the blow. He needed to alert Javi, then find Mia's tools and repair the fence.

"Hayden?" Mia's voice rained down from the deck above. "What's happening?"

He couldn't look up. His head spun and his stomach whirled, possibly from the blow against the piling.

But more likely, because he knew what he was.

A failure.

Once again, he'd failed to protect Mia and her family from life-threatening danger.

Mia wrapped her arms around herself as she leaned against the door frame of Ruthie's room, watching her daughter sleep in the soft glow of the dolphin-shaped night-light Hayden had bought on one of their outings.

The heavy sweatshirt she'd pulled on before she rushed onto the deck was too warm to wear inside, but she felt safer in layers, as though the bulk of the fabric provided protection. It was as foolish as tucking her foot under the blankets to keep the "monsters under the bed" at bay, but she wasn't above psychological self warfare if it helped hold her together.

Male voices drifted from downstairs, low and urgent. Hayden was giving a statement to Javi, but she wasn't sure she wanted the answers to what the horrible noise outside had been, why Hayden had been in the backyard in his pajamas or why he'd called Javi.

And worst of all…why the fire department had arrived to deal with a "gasoline spill."

Her brain did a fabulous job of piecing the images together into a picture of terror. Her imagination worked so well that she'd bolted up the stairs to check on Ruthie, who was sleeping peacefully despite the noise.

She wanted to bar the doors and windows so they'd be

locked inside this house, the one place where she'd always felt nothing bad could reach them.

Mia hugged her stomach tighter. After tonight, she'd never feel that way again.

If she lost the refuge of her home, what did she have left?

"Hey." Hayden's soft whisper washed over her, warmer than her sweatshirt could ever be.

Easing Ruthie's door closed, she turned toward the stairs.

Hayden stood on the top step, his head tilted to one side. The way his eyebrows drew together and his forehead creased, he almost looked confused.

With a last glance at Ruthie's door, Mia stepped softly toward him, avoiding the third plank from the stairs that tended to squeak.

Why bother? Ruthie had slept through the whirling lights and the shouts of first responders. A noisy floorboard was nothing.

When she reached Hayden, he backed down a step. "How's Ruthie?"

"Knocked out." Hayden's presence brought an inexplicable sense of calm. It wasn't just that there was another person standing by her—it was Hayden himself. She'd said something to her mother about that a couple of months earlier, but Mom hadn't commented. She'd just stared at Mia for a long time before smiling the smile Mia remembered from every Christmas Eve of her childhood, as though she carried a special secret.

Of course, that had nothing to do with what was happening now. "Is Javi still here?" The fire trucks had pulled out about ten minutes earlier, but she hadn't heard tires on the gravel drive since.

She liked her driveway. The popping of rocks under tires alerted her when someone pulled up.

Her stomach dropped. Even how she'd graveled her drive spoke of a way to protect herself. How much did fear control her life?

She reached for the handrail to steady herself, and Hayden backed down another step.

Mia frowned, trying to shake a sense that she was dreaming. "Any word on Paige?"

"No, and Javi's gone. The search teams are still out, and the sheriff is putting boats in the water."

"Why boats? What happened out there?"

Tilting his head toward the first floor, Hayden turned to walk downstairs. "I'll make you some tea and we'll talk."

"I don't want tea." She muttered the words, her heart rate picking up as she followed Hayden. Whatever had happened to bring half of the county's emergency personnel to her house must have been bad.

Hayden must have heard her refusal, because he went into the den and turned on the lamp by the couch. He walked to the French doors and stared at the closed blinds.

It was odd that they were closed. Mia sank onto the denim-blue couch and watched Hayden. When he bunked in her living room, he opened the blinds after she went to bed so he could look out at the river. He was a nature guy and hated being cooped up.

His laptop was on the coffee table beside a closed file with a case number on the tab. A piece of paper covered all but the first three numbers, indicating the file was from the state. She didn't want to consider that it might be the details of Keith's murder. Her mind couldn't handle the past when the present was out of control. "What's going on, Hay?"

"There's not an easy or gentle way to say this." He didn't turn from the doors. "Someone tried to burn your house down."

The stark words hit like a bomb. The blow was so hard, she dropped against the back of the couch. "What?" She'd heard him wrong. He had to have said something else, something much less frightening. Maybe she was dreaming. Maybe this whole day had been a nightmare. *Please, let me wake up soon.*

But the pulse in her cheek from impact with the rough bricks in Watchman's Alley said otherwise.

Regret softened Hayden's features. He moved in front of the couch and sat on the coffee table, facing Mia. He clasped his fingers between his knees. Instead of looking directly at her, he looked over her shoulder at the front door. "I should have eased you into that."

"It wouldn't have changed anything." Piled onto the horrors of the day, this new terror in the night exploded like a rocket-propelled grenade. The concussion from the blast was brutal, but eerie silence followed.

Her brain couldn't comprehend. Her emotions couldn't process. She was simply numb. Empty. It was as though she'd stepped out of her life to watch it pass on a movie screen.

Disassociation. A hallmark of the anxiety that had plagued her since the night Keith died.

Exhaling through pursed lips, she sat up taller. "Tell me what happened."

Hayden slid until the backs of his knees touched the table. He pressed his palms against the rough wood on either side of his knees and wrapped his fingers around it, gripping so hard that his knuckles turned white. "I had the blinds open, and I saw someone in the yard." He quickly recapped the confrontation with a man who'd poured gasoline around her home's support pillars before fighting with Hayden and escaping in a boat.

It was as though he was telling someone else's story. It

didn't compute that this was happening to her...to Ruthie. The *why* eluded her. She tried to piece together facts, but nothing made sense. "That's why the sheriff put boats on the river."

Hayden nodded.

Mia stared at the French doors as though she could see the river on the other side. "It's too late. That man is long gone. He could have tucked into a little cove, could be all the way out to the sound. It's a waste of energy. Sheriff Davidson should let everyone go home and sleep. They're all probably already exhausted from searching for Paige."

"No one would take him up on the offer. You're family, and they're going to do their best to stop someone from doing this to one of their own."

The words brought a lump to her throat. Her next breath was a whimper. Tears stung her eyes. She stared at Hayden's chest, unable to look him in the face. "Well, I don't feel like one of them anymore." Since panic attacks had forced her out of her job four years earlier, she'd felt like a wanderer and an outcast. The deputies visited and offered encouraging words, but those things smacked of pity. Hayden made it sound like they wanted to help, like they still truly cared.

Their concern squeezed her heart. It also made her feel like a giant burden. A bother. An added weight to men and women who were already overextended and had families of their own to care for.

Hayden's exhale almost sounded like defeat. Slowly, as though he was afraid she might reach across the gap and punch him, he laid his hand on hers. "Let them do this for you." His grip tightened. "It makes you feel helpless when you see someone you care about suffering. They need to be on the move for you and Ruthie."

"I'm not good at this." The panic attacks had driven a need for control deep into her soul. She hated asking for help. Hated releasing things to other people. She should be able to take care of everything by herself. To protect her daughter, her home…

Yet she couldn't. Everything was violently *out* of control, spinning like a hurricane, threatening to destroy what was left of her fragile existence.

She sniffed, staring at Hayden's hand covering hers. The unknowns rushed in, crowding her mind while her emotions remained untouched. Still, her brain knew what she *should* be feeling. "Hay, I'm scared."

"I know." His low words calmed her thoughts, allowing rationality to take over.

She pressed her feet against the floor, trying to ground herself. "Somebody's targeting me. They know how to get to me and to Ruthie."

Hayden tensed. After a long moment in which he seemed to hold his breath, he let go of her hand, then moved to sit beside her, resting his shoulder against hers. "I won't let that happen."

The words shuddered through Mia, both comforting and chilling.

Comforting because she wasn't alone. *Chilling* because standing in the gap for her just might get Hayden killed.

FIVE

What was he thinking?

As Mia leaned her shoulder against his, Hayden wrestled with dueling urges. Half of him wanted to put his arm around her, shielding her from the world while reassuring himself that she was safe. The other half wanted to pull away and sit on the far side of the room to escape the wave of longing that roared through him at her touch. This was something he'd never felt with her before, and it was *not* what either of them needed. Not now, not ever.

Mia breathed deeply, her shoulder sliding against his. "What now?"

How did he answer that question? *What now* with the threat outside? Or *what now* with this weird feeling? He'd never kept anything from Mia before. She was his closest friend. Although he'd hugged her and comforted her many times, he'd never wanted to hold her close and never let go. Not like this.

No. He shouldn't be feeling like he needed her as much as she needed him. Wasn't he supposed to be the strong one here? And wasn't she Keith's wife?

"Hayden?" She pulled away to see his face, then turned toward him. "Are you hurt? I didn't even ask—"

"I'm fine." The words were gruffer than he'd intended, but it had taken a lot of force to get the sound out without choking. He cleared his throat. "I'm not hurt. The couple of blows he landed weren't bad."

"You're sure? Because you and I are about to have some twin facial bruises." She reached out to touch his cheek, where he'd just realized a pulsing pain had set in.

But if she touched him…

He jumped up and went to the doors, lifting a slat on the blinds and looking into the darkness.

Thankfully, Mia stayed on the couch.

He shoved his hands into the pockets of his flannel pants and balled his fists. She'd asked a question, and he needed to get out of his feelings enough to answer.

If only he *had* an answer. "What comes next? I don't know." When he faced her, he focused on the front door, which she'd painted a deep blue to contrast with the white walls. "I don't think you can stay here, though." She wasn't going to like that. This house was her anchor. Moving her to another location would pile on the trauma for her and likely for Ruthie as well, especially since they were knocking on the door of Christmas.

Mia flinched, the motion obvious even in his peripheral vision. "The tactical part of me won't stop spinning a plan. Pack up. Get out. Find somewhere safe where this guy can't get to Ruthie or me. But the other part of me…"

When her voice faded, Hayden let his gaze slide to her.

She fiddled with the hem of her shirt. "The weak part of me is scared."

The jagged confession shredded his heart. Whatever feelings his mind was inventing due to fear and exhaustion, he needed to set it all aside. She needed him.

With a quick prayer, Hayden locked a lid on his roaring emotions and sat beside her. He wrapped his arm around her shoulder and drew her to his side, the action raising an ache deep in his chest. "This fear isn't weakness. After what's happened to you today, it's normal. Fight or flight. Your body is prepping you for one or the other. Any living, breathing human would be processing this the same way you are."

"Maybe." When she shook her head, the motion brushed her hair against his shoulder. "I don't want fight or flight, though. I want option C. Hide in my house and pretend nothing is happening." She chuckled bitterly. "I'd definitely call that *weak*."

If he could take all of this away, he would. He'd fly them to the moon, hide them behind the stars that dotted the sky.

But that was impossible. The fight was here, and they both knew it. "You are the strongest person I know. No discussion. Stop calling my favorite person *weak*." He squeezed her shoulder. "Right now, you don't have to think about anything. You can let go for a few minutes. I'm right here, and I'm going to make sure nothing else happens." He wasn't alone. A couple of other off duty deputies were hanging out on the fringes of the yard. He'd never tell her that, because she'd fall into a guilt spiral and tell them to go home. "I'm not going anywhere." He'd die first. "I'll figure this out. You rest."

"Thank you." Her whisper was barely audible. Hayden felt it in her breathing more than he heard it with his ears.

Gradually, her breaths fell into a rhythm, and her head rested heavier on his shoulder. In spite of everything, she'd dropped off to sleep.

Hayden didn't dare move. He let his head fall to the back of the couch and stared at the ceiling, trying to unravel the knots in his thinking. The tangles had nothing to do with the danger around Mia and Ruthie.

No, this was much worse.

Mia had been one of his closest friends since she started dating Keith in middle school. She'd never needed a defender.

She'd been as strong in body and spirit as any of the guys. She'd also been Keith's girlfriend and therefore Hayden's de facto "little sister," so he'd looked out for her. When they'd both joined the sheriff's department, she'd been his coworker, and they'd have defended one another to the death. In those days, he'd been engaged to Beth, and their group of four had fallen into an easy rhythm as couple friends, "doing life together," as their preacher liked to say.

When Ruthie was born, Hayden had learned what it truly meant to want to protect someone with his life. The honor of being her godfather had been a natural fit, and he'd taken the responsibility seriously. If anything had happened to Keith and Mia, it would have been up to him and Beth to teach Ruthie how to navigate the world and to know God. He'd been "Uncle Hayden" from the moment the little girl could form words.

Of course, Beth had been gone before Ruthie learned to speak. She'd walked away, unable to deal with Hayden's grief over his best friend's violent murder.

Hayden's jaw tightened.

Keith's murder had solidified his protector role in Mia's and Ruthie's lives. The need to shield them from the world and to help in any way he could had driven him since that moment.

But something different had hit him this evening as he'd stood at the top of the stairs watching Mia. Something terrifying. Something he could honestly say he'd never felt before, not even with his fiancée.

He needed Mia. Somehow, she made him whole.

When he'd walked up the stairs, he hadn't expected her to be standing at Ruthie's door. The sight of her had stopped him. She'd wrapped her arms around her stomach, digging her hands into her heavy sweatshirt as though it was armor that could protect her from the world. Her entire being radiated vulnerability.

But that hadn't been the thing that struck him so hard he'd nearly run down the stairs and bolted out into the night.

No, rather than feeling the need to protect her, his own vulnerability had risen up. While he'd wanted to take care of her the way he always had, a deeper need had surged from his stomach into his chest. He *needed* to pull her close and to feel her breathe, to hold her in his arms, not because he wanted to keep her safe, but because he wanted to draw strength from her. To be comforted by her as much as he comforted her.

Mia had become his safe place.

He closed his eyes as the truth assailed him. On days when work was tough or he felt as though he'd failed yet again, he called her. On days when he had something to celebrate, he called her. On days when he was bored or sad or simply had the best burger he'd ever eaten in his life and wanted to share the joy, he called her. Mia knew his best and his worst in ways Beth never had.

At some point, this friendship had shifted. He'd always thought he was the strong one who helped to steer the ship around the shoals and piloted it through storms, but the truth was, Mia anchored him.

This can't be happening, Lord. He fired off a desperate prayer. *Mia is Keith's wife. You didn't give her to me. You gave her to him. You gave me the responsibility of keeping her safe, of helping her out, not...not of feeling things for her. This is wrong. Make it go away. Please.*

The prayer only unsettled him more. It dropped into his stomach and smoldered, burning so hot that it made his abs clinch.

He should pull away, physically and emotionally. Even right now, he should slip his arm from around her and walk away. He shouldn't stay here resting in the feel of Mia in his arms as though it was right and real.

But he couldn't. He was the first line of defense, the *only* line of defense, between Mia and Ruthie and whoever was coming at them. He was a constant in Ruthie's life, and he wouldn't walk away from that little girl. That would make him no better than Beth.

He couldn't walk away from Mia, either. He might as well rip his heart out of his chest and leave it beating on her hardwood floor.

He groaned, the rumble low in his chest. What he ought to do was—

A low, repetitive buzz sounded to his right. His phone screen lit up where he'd laid it on the couch an arm's length away.

Trying not to jostle Mia, he reached until his fingertips brushed the screen, then dragged the device closer.

The text was from Javi.

Keeping the phone next to his thigh to prevent the light from waking Mia, he flicked the screen and keyed in his passcode.

A message popped up, dousing the burn in his stomach with icy water. Body found in river. Female. ID pending.

Hayden pressed his lips together tightly to hold in an anguished groan. He prayed it wasn't so, but his gut said this was the end none of them wanted.

His gut said Paige was dead.

Mia cradled her coffee cup in her palms and walked across the dark kitchen to the bay window, where she stared at the closed blinds. Blue light filtered around the slats, indicating the softening of darkness just before sunrise.

Darkness was her enemy. Daylight was her friend.

As much as she welcomed the dawn, it was too early to be

awake. Mia sipped the black coffee that Hayden had made during the night, then tilted her head from side to side, trying to loosen the tightness in her neck.

She'd awakened around five, muscles stiff and mind fuzzy, her neck awkwardly resting on the couch cushion. Hayden was racked out in the chair across from her, his feet propped on the coffee table. He'd moved at some point during the night, probably to get more comfortable.

He'd be hurting worse than her when he got moving. Maybe it was a good thing she'd invested in the big bottle of ibuprofen from the warehouse store. Aging was no fun for "normal" people. It was a lot worse for someone like her. Although she was only in her early thirties, raging anxiety had forced entirely too much tension into her body.

The hardwood behind her creaked. Her hand jerked, sloshing coffee over her wrist. It took half a second for her mind to remember she wasn't alone. "Did you get decent sleep?"

When she turned, Hayden stood in the entry, hair rumpled and face saggy from sleep. The lines around his eyes were deep with exhaustion. Somehow, he still exuded strength and safety.

And he didn't look half bad, either.

Something deep in Mia's chest tweaked, almost like her heart skipped. She looked at the black coffee still making waves in her mug. Yeah, she probably needed less of that. Or maybe she needed more if her brain had decided to be attracted to Hayden for even one of those extra beats. He was her closest friend.

He was *Keith's* closest friend.

If her weary heart wanted to pound an extra beat at the sight of Hayden McGrath, it could get itself into line. She was never exposing her heart to be shattered again.

Maybe she needed a pacemaker. There was no doubt she

was old before her time. The past few years had aged her immeasurably.

The lines around Hayden's eyes deepened.

Mia set her mug on the counter, concerned. "Are you okay?"

"Yeah." He shook his head as though he was shaking off a spiderweb, then scrubbed the top of his head, rumpling his hair even further. "Do I look that bad? You're staring like I've got the cooties Ruthie is always talking about."

Mia snorted. "You look like you slept in a chair. How's your neck?"

"Probably the same as yours. Ibuprofen is still in the cabinet by the sink?" He headed that way before she could respond.

"Yeah, but you might want to eat before you pop one." While she used to down them dry on an empty stomach when she was in the army, age and wisdom had taught her she felt a whole lot better if she gave the meds a cushion to land on.

Hayden looked over his shoulder as he opened the cabinet door. "You getting old, Galloway? Losing your army toughness?" He popped two and swallowed them without breaking eye contact. "*Hooah*, Sergeant."

In spite of the tension, a laugh bubbled up. "It's your gut, soldier." She lifted her mug. "I turned the burner back on, so the coffee's warm. There's cereal and breakfast bars, or I can make eggs." Ruthie was on a cheese omelet kick, so eggs and shredded cheddar were in plentiful supply.

"I'll wait and eat with the kid." He poured a cup of coffee, seeming to be in constant motion. "How'd you sleep?"

"Like a baby." Sarcasm dripped from her words. "Waking up frequently all night long. What time did you pass out?"

"No idea. Probably a couple of hours ago. I wasn't planning on falling asleep, but..." He shrugged, sipped his coffee and then walked toward the living room, making a wide berth around her. "We need to talk about a plan."

Mia's chin dropped to her chest. She left her coffee on the table to prevent her shaking hands from soaking her wrist again. He wasn't telling her anything she didn't already know, but she'd prefer to act like this was a normal Sunday. Like she was going to get Ruthie dressed, then head to church, where they'd sit with Paige and her family before coming home for lunch with friends who understood that she wasn't always a fan of crowded restaurants.

She had two truly safe places. One was this house. The other was her church. Today, both were being ripped away. As much as she wanted to make like an ostrich and stick her head in the sand, she needed to face reality.

Someone wanted to harm her, which meant Ruthie was in danger as well. Even if she lacked the energy to protect herself, mama bear needed to make sure her daughter was safe.

This was harder than she'd expected. Although she spent time with God every day, church was a boost to her system. Without it, she felt weak and lost.

She also felt trapped. As sunrise pinked the light around the blinds, she longed to open them as she always did. Flooding the house with light would boot out the darkness.

She settled for lifting a slat and peering out into the new day.

Movement near the fence jerked her hand back, the slat rattling into place.

Someone was out there.

Her hands shook. She should alert Hayden, but his name stuck in her throat. She peeked out again to watch the shadowy figure, trying to determine the severity of the threat.

The man walked toward her, his gaze on the fence before he turned his face toward the sky.

A familiar face.

Mia let the blinds fall, then stalked into the living room, where Hayden stood in front of the French doors with one set of blinds open, watching the sky brighten. "Hay, why is Deputy Gallagher in my yard?"

Hayden sipped his coffee as though Drew Gallagher wandered around her yard every morning. "He's keeping an eye on the perimeter to the north and east. Peña is walking the west and south."

Mia sagged, her shoulder braced against the frame of the large opening between the kitchen and living room. "Amelia Peña was on duty yesterday, and I know for a fact she's got a shift today, because last week she told me she wouldn't be at church. She should be home asleep. And the Gallaghers have a three-month-old. His wife needs—"

"Don't you dare go out there and run them off." Hayden's voice held the weight of authority. "They volunteered to stay. We talked about this last night. Be grateful, not guilty."

Mia's jaw dropped, but she forced it closed as she straightened. He had no idea what it was like to be her. No one should sacrifice for her, not when she couldn't offer anything in return.

Amelia needed to take care of herself, to rest between shifts. Drew should be home with Cassidy and their precious baby, not shivering on patrol in her backyard. She was no more special than anyone else who needed help.

Hayden could tell her all day not to feel guilty, but it wasn't going to change anything. "They don't need to do this. Neither do you." She was keeping him from his life. He was here way too often, taking Ruthie on outings or doing things around the house, offering emotional support and carrying some of her burden.

Hayden was a handsome guy, one who turned heads, especially when he'd worn a uniform. While his dark hair now sported a few threads of gray, it only served to make him more attract—

Mia shuddered. *Nope.* That was the second time in ten minutes that she'd headed down that road. *Why?*

She had no idea. The point was… "They have lives. You have a life. You've been stuck ever since Keith died, taking care of me and Ruthie. You should be…" She waved her hand toward somewhere out there. "You should be taking care of your own life. Finding a woman who loves you. Settling into—"

"I'm fine." The words snapped. "My life is exactly what I want it to be." He didn't look directly at her, a habit he seemed to have picked up in the past twelve hours. "And everyone else? They care about you. They care about Ruthie. You wore the uniform with them, and you're still one of them. They feel just as helpless as—" His brow furrowed. "They want to help you. Let them. You've given so much to each of them. You're their family. They're your family. Don't wound them by fussing at them instead of thanking them."

"I haven't given anybody anything." She sank onto a bar stool by the kitchen entrance and threw her hands into the air, ashamed of her impotence. "All I do is take." That was the worst part of the PTSD-induced panic attacks that drove her into a near reclusiveness. She could no longer have anybody's back. All of her energy went to staying alive and raising her daughter. By the time night fell, she was exhausted, but sleep had ceased to be her friend so the cycle never ended.

"Mia." Hayden exhaled her name, then stepped around the couch to stand in front of her. Reaching around her, he settled his coffee on the counter, his chest brushing her nose.

He smelled like coffee and…well, like Hayden. She closed

her eyes and breathed him in, not bothering to consider why his presence had a different feel today.

When he backed away, he rested his hands on her shoulders. "You really have no idea, do you?" The words were soft.

Mia stared at the stylized mountain logo on his sweatshirt. Something cautioned her against looking him in the eye. He was standing so close, and it was…different. Comforting but different. Charged. Magnetic.

"People love you because they choose to. They help because they want to. And, Mia?" He hooked his finger under her chin and gently forced her to meet his gaze. "You opened your home to Amelia when she first took this job and was looking for a place to live. You cooked a billion freezer meals for the Gallaghers when the baby was born."

"That was nothing." It hadn't taken much effort to do those things.

His gaze was intense, searching hers. "You don't see your own value, do you?"

What value? She had nothing to give.

But somehow, with Hayden looking at her the way he was right now, with a wonder she'd never seen before, she felt treasured. Special. Like maybe she had something to share…with him?

The realization jolted, and she jerked away from him, scrambling off the stool and deeper into the kitchen, her mind spinning. "I'll… I could at least make them fresh coffee."

Hayden stayed where he was, seeming to be frozen, until a buzzing sound forced his hand to his pocket. He glanced at his phone, and his jaw hardened.

Something was wrong. "Hayden?"

His eyes were dark. It was clear he wished he could say something different than what he was about to say. "They found Paige."

SIX

"This is the exact last place you should be." Hayden killed the truck's engine and leaned over the steering wheel as he surveyed the front of the two-story white house where Paige had grown up.

The home was situated in the center of a tree-covered lot, isolated from the road. A half dozen cars were parked along the edges of the winding driveway.

Paige was a popular member of their church. The kids all loved her and so did the adults. Her family was well respected in Wincombe. They wouldn't lack for support on this darkest of days.

"Are you listening to me, Mia?"

They were not getting into this conversation in front of her daughter. Mia stared at Hayden until he looked at her, then she cut her eyes toward the back seat of his pickup, where Ruthie played happily with his phone. This was hard enough without Hayden questioning her every three seconds.

It had taken every ounce of her rapidly dwindling reserves to pack bags for her and Ruthie and to hold it together on the short drive to Paige's family home. As soon as they made this stop at the Crosbys', they were headed to Hayden's house about an hour away, near Elizabeth City.

It was a risky move, but Hayden felt they'd be safer out of town.

Right now, nowhere felt safe. Her home was compromised. The routine she depended on was shattered. She wasn't in church. She wasn't making last-minute preparations for Christmas, just a few days away.

Instead she was offering condolences to her daughter's birth family, then fleeing the threat that had likely killed their youngest child.

Anxiety often made her feel like she stared at life from the outside, but this level of surreal was something she hadn't felt since the initial weeks after Keith's murder.

A gray sedan tucked in close to the pickup's bumper. Two of Hayden's Trinity teammates had arrived while Hayden was loading the truck, but they hadn't come into the house. All she knew was that one man and one woman were acting as her bodyguards.

How had this become her life? Wasn't it bad enough that her husband had been murdered? Now Paige was dead, and both she and Ruthie were targets?

Swallowing fear that threatened to choke her, Mia slid her gaze to Hayden. *Focus on the moment.* It was the only way to survive. "I know this is ill-advised." Although protecting herself and Ruthie was top priority, she couldn't leave without seeing Paige's mother. Sue Crosby, her daughter, Eve, and son-in-law, Daniel, were basically family. In the wake of tragedy, she couldn't simply disappear.

She might be living a life that had slipped off its foundation, but she wasn't built to ignore hurting people. Guilt would kill her before fear or an assailant got the chance.

"Ill-advised?" Hayden scoffed. "That's an understatement." He'd been irritable and distant since they'd received word of Paige's death.

Paige. All Hayden had told her was that Ruthie's birth mother had suffered a blow to the head. With the holidays, it would take a while before the coroner made an official report. Even at that, Hayden was keeping something from her. He was rarely this moody. While she understood, she needed him to offer her some stability.

Mia winced. Could she be more selfish? She wasn't the only one grieving. Hayden had to feel pain as well. And Paige's family... "I have to do this." She stared out the window at the pine trees.

Her life had already been marred by violence. She could understand what the Crosbys were enduring. While the idea of stepping into that crowded house without knowing the identity of Paige's killer twisted her stomach into knots, she couldn't stay away.

Hayden's hand wrapped around hers, warm and comforting. "I don't like it, but I understand, and I'm sorry for being snappy. I'll walk you to the door, then take Ruthie around back to the tire swing."

Mia nodded. She'd chosen not to tell Ruthie what had happened until things calmed down. The little girl adored her "Pai-pai," as she'd called Paige from toddlerhood. Although she was too young to understand the true nature of their relationship, the death of her birth mother would devastate Ruthie. Combined with leaving home just a few days before Christmas, this might be more than her daughter could handle.

They'd simply told Ruthie that Pai-pai wasn't home and she could play outside while Mommy talked to the grown-ups. Because she loved the tire swing in the backyard, she'd happily agreed.

"Have Sue text me when you're ready to leave, and I'll

meet you on the porch. No more detours after this. Even with an escort, I'm not excited about having you in the open."

Ignoring the hint of danger, Mia walked to the house, her heart pounding. When Hayden left her at the door, it took all she had not to beg him to go inside with her. She needed his support, his presence. She felt exposed as she pressed the doorbell.

The door immediately swung open, and Sue Crosby enveloped her in a hug. "Mia." The older woman broke into sobs as Mia returned the embrace.

As she eased Sue inside and tapped the door closed with her foot, the band around Mia's lungs loosened. The biggest lesson she'd learned about panic attacks was that when she focused on the needs of someone else, the walk became a little easier. Although she was drowning in grief and fear, reaching out to Sue eased those emotions, if only for a moment.

There would be time to fall apart later. Right now, Paige's mother needed her. They stood in the foyer, Sue weeping as Mia comforted her.

No one came upon them there, although indistinct voices drifted from the kitchen at the rear of the house.

When the storm subsided, Sue swiped at her face. "I was hoping you'd come." She sniffed and looked to the side, toward the formal living room. "Who would do this? Are you and Ruthie safe? The sheriff said there was an incident—"

"I don't know." Oh, how she wished she did.

Sue frowned, then fluffed her hair as though she was putting herself back in order. In her midfifties, Sue's brown hair was streaked with silver and, even in her grief, perfectly in place. She was always put together, even in the midst of her world falling apart. After a glance toward the kitchen, she looked at Mia, her expression gentle. "The family is here, along with a few of Paige's friends. Do you want to speak to them or is that too much?"

As a social worker for the school system, Sue understood the psychological battles Mia faced. Sue had been a confidant during their fertility journey and an advocate during Ruthie's adoption. Together they'd built a sort of blended family that benefited Ruthie, particularly in the wake of Keith's death. They needed one another now more than ever, yet she was packing up Ruthie and running away.

Was it the right thing to do?

What choice did she have? She'd offer comfort while she was here, but then she had to consider Ruthie's safety above all else. She waved her hand for Sue to lead the way up the short hallway. "Is Cade here?"

Cade Crosby was Sue's ex-husband and Paige's father. He'd been the lone voice of dissension during the adoption discussions, wanting Paige and her ex-boyfriend Blake to "own up" to their "mistakes," to drop out of college and raise Ruthie themselves. He lived several hours away near Wilmington and rarely visited. When he did, he radiated disapproval.

Sue stopped in front of the closed kitchen door. "Cade is upstairs in Paige's room. He's not ready to see anyone. He needs time, and I doubt he comes downstairs, but Mia…" She winced. "Blake is here."

Mia turned toward the backyard where Ruthie was playing, though she couldn't see anything from the windowless hallway.

Ruthie hadn't seen her birth father since the day she was born. While Paige was fully involved in Ruthie's life, Blake had made it clear that it was easier for him emotionally to step away. He'd willingly consented to the adoption and had never expressed regret. Although he'd remained friends with

Paige after they broke up, he'd maintained a respectful distance from Mia and Ruthie.

Mia rarely saw him, since he lived in Greenville near the college. The few times they'd spoken, it had been awkward. She never knew what to say. The tiniest part of her wondered if he resented their family.

"Should he be here?" As her ex-boyfriend, he'd be among the first the police questioned.

Sue clearly picked up on the real question. "He spoke with the police already. He has an alibi but, Mia, I'd never suspect him. He cared too much about her to harm her."

Mia wanted to believe so, but her nature was to suspect everyone. The world wasn't safe.

This would be easier with Hayden beside her, but there were some things she needed to do alone. With a swift prayer, she followed Sue into the kitchen. She was here to support Paige's family, not to be a burden.

The dozen or so people scattered around the island and the breakfast nook in the large, airy kitchen were somber, talking in low tones. When Mia appeared, the conversation ebbed, but it picked up again when Paige's older sister, Eve, approached with her husband, Daniel.

Eve hugged Mia, then stepped back under her husband's arm. "I'm glad you came. Mom was wondering if you'd—" She leaned more heavily on her husband. "Is Ruthie here?"

"She's outside with Hayden. We're…" Should she say something? "We're going to go somewhere and lay low for a bit."

Daniel nodded, his expression drawn. "That makes sense. This thing is so… I can't believe it all." He offered a tight smile. "I'd been hoping to take Ruthie fishing if the weather warmed up."

"Hopefully we'll be back soon." Ruthie loved fishing with Daniel and had gone several times with him and Hayden.

"If you're going to be here a second, we'll run to the house and get Ruthie's Christmas present. It's this talking globe that you connect to your phone and it does all of these augmented reality things." She smiled up at her husband. "Very tech."

Glad for the distraction, Mia smiled. "I'm not surprised." Daniel worked in IT for the state's Department of Natural Resources. He'd been a college classmate of Keith's and had met Eve through him.

"We'll be quick." Eve grabbed Daniel, and they slipped out of the kitchen.

Why was she taking her daughter away at Christmas? There had to be another way, right?

In her heart, she knew there wasn't.

She scanned the room, searching for Sue, who'd vanished.

Near the sink, Blake leaned against the counter. His expression was dark, and he stared at the far side of the room without seeming to see anything. The grief radiating off him was palpable. Her heart ached for him, and she started to cross over to speak to him, but Sue approached with a couple in their fifties.

Sue, her red eyes the only thing that betrayed her overwhelming grief, drew Mia closer. "This is Amanda Rhinehart. She was Paige's professor in some of her undergraduate classes and has been mentoring her as she's moved through the master's process."

"I've heard your name many times." Mia hugged the woman. "Paige looked up to you."

Amanda offered a watery smile. "This is my husband, Trent. He works for the college as well, in the Office of Student Financial Aid."

The man appeared to be as grief-stricken as his wife. He

extended his hand to Mia and shook it warmly. "You adopted Paige's daughter?"

Mia flinched internally. What an odd way to address her. She nodded slowly, unsure how to proceed.

Trent studied her for a moment before he dropped her hand. His eyes drifted over her shoulder, creasing with concern.

Mia turned to follow his gaze.

Blake was watching them, his expression dark and angry. He stared for a long moment, then stalked out of the room, violently shoving through the hallway door.

Sue's face registered sympathy. "I'll check on him." She followed Blake out the still-swinging door.

Amanda watched them go. "I hope everything is okay."

Was it? Because Blake's expression said he could be consumed by more than grief. His expression had spoken of anger...

Anger that had seemed to be directed at her.

"Spin me again, Uncle Hayden!" Ruthie's feet were straight out from her perch in the old motorcycle tire tied to the high branch of a pine tree. She gripped the tire's sides as she giggled.

Hayden looked up the sloped yard toward the house, where someone occasionally passed the kitchen window, but he was too far away to discern more than figures. Being away from Mia while a threat hung over their heads made him antsy.

Worse, thickening clouds blocked the sun and cast deep shadows among the trees around the house, offering too many dark places to hide. The wind was picking up, and the movement of limbs and branches created the optical illusion that someone was prowling through the woods.

His adrenaline ran high.

Still, it was nothing compared to the seismic shift his emotions had endured earlier that morning, just before the call about Paige had come in. The same emotions that had distracted him ever since and had made him snap at Mia in the truck.

He'd been overwhelmed in her kitchen by something he hadn't felt in years.

Overwhelmed, swamped, wiped out by the urge to wrap his arms around Mia and to kiss her in a way that let her know how much he needed her. That she wasn't a burden to him. That he might just be in—

"Uncle Hayden!" Ruthie's shout pierced his thoughts at the same moment her tiny sneakered foot caught him in the thigh. "Spin me again!"

He winced at the sharp pain. *Wow.* He needed to get his head out of his heart. If he didn't, he was in far more danger than a small bruise from a tiny foot.

Focusing on the physical pain, he drew himself into the moment with his goddaughter. "You have manners, little miss. We say *please*. And we don't kick people."

"Sorry. And *please* spin me again?" Big hazel eyes looked up at him with every ounce of puppy dog expression that Ruthie could muster.

Hayden glanced at his watch. It had been over ten minutes since they'd arrived, and he was anxious to get moving, but he couldn't drag Ruthie into the house. He'd promised Mia he'd keep the little girl away from the grief of Paige's family until they could find a way to explain what had happened.

With a sigh, he pasted on a smile and looked down at his favorite kid. "You feeling okay?" The way she whirled and twirled through life, he doubted she would ever suffer from motion sickness, but he wanted to be sure before he set the tire swing into another wild spin.

"Yes! Again!" Ruthie's shriek could pierce eardrums.

He winced. "Hold on tight." He slowly turned the tire, twisting the rope into mini knots. "Ready?" At Ruthie's enthusiastic nod, he released the tire. It spun wildly as the rope unwound.

Ruthie laughed and shouted with excited delight.

"Hayden?" At the sound of a voice, he looked over his shoulder to find Gavin Mercer approaching. The dark-haired former CID investigator's hand rested on his hip near his side, where he carried a Glock on the rare occasions he was armed. "Everything okay back here? Rebecca and I heard Ruthie scream."

Behind Gavin, Rebecca Campbell appeared at the corner of the house.

Gratitude for his Trinity team washed through Hayden, easing some of his anxiety. Gavin and Rebecca had left home on their day off to come and back him up, offering security and peace of mind as he moved Ruthie and Mia out of town. He was certain they were ready to get going as much as he was.

None of them were trained bodyguards, though they were all prior military and had some experience in pulling security. Their main specialty was investigations, and they'd been well trained to pick up on details other people might not notice. That attention to detail should give them an edge in surveillance, helping them to see things coming that untrained eyes might miss.

"We're fine." He tilted his head toward Ruthie, who giggled loudly as the spinning tire slowed. "Somebody is hopefully going to take a nice nap once we get moving."

Rebecca walked down the hill to join them, her brown ponytail swinging with her steps. "I'm taking notes. My sister's kid is due in a few months."

"And you're planning to be the best aunt ever?" Gavin elbowed her arm.

"You know it. I'll be spoiling that kid rotten." Rebecca grinned, then glanced at her watch and sobered. "How much longer do you think Mia will be?"

"Hopefully not much." Hayden held up a hand to press pause on the questions, then walked over and twisted the tire in the opposite direction. Maybe a reversal would counteract any dizziness and keep Ruthie from falling over when they walked back to the truck. "One last time, Ruthie. Are you ready?"

"Yes!"

As soon as she gave the affirmative, Hayden let go of the tire and stepped back to rejoin Rebecca and Gavin. Ruthie should be sufficiently distracted for at least sixty seconds. "I may go in and get her if she's not out soon, if you guys can keep Ruthie occupied. The longer we stay here, the more time and opportunity we give for someone to make another run at them. I won't feel easy until we're settled in at our destination." He was careful not to say where they were headed. There could be listening ears. While it wouldn't be hard to figure out where he lived, he didn't want to make it easier for someone to find them.

"Copy that." Gavin backed up a few steps toward the house. "I'll go to the car and make sure we're ready to roll."

Hayden nodded and turned to Rebecca. "I'll get Mia if you'll keep an eye on Ruthie."

"On it." She stepped around him to walk closer to Ruthie, who was kicking her legs as she spun. "And I'll watch out for flying feet."

"They hurt." Hayden chuckled and rubbed his thigh, then followed Gavin up the hill. He stopped a few feet behind his teammate as Gavin slowed at the corner of the house. "If we can get on the road in the next ten minutes, then—"

The words died as Gavin drew his pistol, then turned and motioned Hayden forward, anger reddening his face. Hayden rushed to his teammate's side, fear and helplessness swimming in his stomach. Whatever Gavin saw, it upset him. Worse, Hayden was unarmed, having left his pistol locked up at his house, never dreaming he'd need it in Wincombe.

When he reached Gavin, his teammate didn't turn away from what he was watching. "Text Mia. Tell her to stay inside." His voice was barely a whisper.

"Can't. We left her phone to prevent being tracked." In hindsight, that might have been a bad idea.

Gavin muttered something under his breath. With two fingers, he pointed at the driveway where their vehicles were parked.

Although Hayden's truck largely blocked their view, blue-jeaned legs were visible beneath the truck near the tailgate where a person had crouched on their knees.

Someone was tampering with his truck.

Hayden's blood ran cold. This was a monumental failure on his part. He should have insisted they go straight out of town. Should have told Rebecca and Gavin to stay with the vehicles. Should have done so many things differently.

Gavin leaned forward, trying to get a better line of sight. "How do you want to handle this?"

Regardless of how wrongly he'd played this from the start, the opportunity to catch the person terrorizing Mia and Ruthie now lay before him. Swallowing his self-recrimination, Hayden laid a hand on Gavin's shoulder. "We end this. Now."

SEVEN

Hayden stared at the legs of the person behind his truck. While he wanted to charge forward and tackle the suspect, priority number one was getting Ruthie to safety and keeping Mia from stepping outside.

While Gavin kept watch, Hayden fired off a text to Rebecca. Get Ruthie inside. Tell Mia to stay put. Don't alarm anyone. While everyone should shelter in place, the last thing the Crosby family needed was to be alerted that Paige's killer might be on their property.

After all, this could be a huge misunderstanding.

He wasn't sure if he hoped this was a false alarm or if he wanted this to be a full-blown threat so they could stop the madness.

Tapping Gavin on the shoulder, Hayden held up his empty hands to indicate he was unarmed. At Gavin's nod, Hayden pointed to the right, then aimed his finger at himself before swinging it to the left. They had no way of knowing if the person was armed, so as the one with a weapon, Gavin would approach from the front while Hayden operated with the element of surprise and moved in from the rear.

This thrown-together plan had better work.

With a deep breath and a quick prayer, Hayden signaled a silent order for Gavin to proceed.

Gavin stayed below the house's window level as he crept past the porch. While there wasn't a lot of cover, he was at an angle that their target couldn't spot him unless they stood.

Hayden gave his teammate a few seconds' head start, then he crouched and darted from his position to the far side of the nearest vehicle, a full-size SUV. He'd have to move quickly through the gaps between cars, navigating several feet of open space each time where he could easily be spotted.

He rushed from the cover of the large SUV to a smaller crossover, then stopped. He was directly across the wide gravel drive from his pickup, but there was a vehicle-length gap between the crossover and the sedan that was next in line.

Someone had left the house since they'd arrived. How had he not heard a vehicle leave down the gravel drive? Why hadn't Gavin or Rebecca said something? Likely it was innocent, but he should have been aware of it.

He swallowed the burn that tried to rise in his throat. He'd been too distracted with keeping Ruthie occupied, and he'd missed sights and sounds that could have indicated potential danger. He had to do better.

That included honing his focus now.

Hayden eased back along the side of the crossover to the hood and raised his head to look for Gavin. Rather than risk being spotted as he moved between the crossover and the sedan, he'd have to make his move from the side instead of from the rear.

Gavin was hidden, so Hayden couldn't signal the change in plan. Guess they'd have to go with the flow.

At the crossover's rear bumper, Hayden took up a runner's crouch, ready to dart out as soon as he heard Gavin's shout.

Blood raced through his veins. This could be it. This could be—

Gavin's voice broke the stillness. "Got a runner!"

Hayden leaped from his concealed position and dashed into the driveway. Following Gavin, he dove into the woods, dodging tree branches and trying not to trip over roots in the thick vegetation.

Ahead of them, the shadows were deep on the cloud-soaked day, and they danced with the wind. The damp air that promised rain threatened to suffocate him, but he pushed forward, following Gavin and the sounds of someone crashing through the trees ahead of them, though he had no visual on the person they were chasing.

His breath came in heavy gasps. A side stitch threatened to take him down, but he pushed on. This was for Mia. For Ruthie.

For Paige. For Keith.

Gavin stopped so suddenly that Hayden nearly crashed into his back. Holding up his hands, he stopped himself by bracing against Gavin's shoulder blades. "What?"

"Lost him."

Around them, the woods had fallen silent. No footsteps on leaves. No breaking of branches. The only sound was their breathing, and the only movement was the wind tangling the tree branches above them. It was as though the person they were chasing had disappeared. "How?"

Gavin stepped a few feet ahead, scanning left and right, then returned to Hayden's side. "I don't know, but as much as we'd both love to charge forward…"

He didn't need to finish the thought. They had no idea what they were heading into. The suspect could be armed. Could have backup. They could race deeper into the woods, straight into death.

While Hayden had made his peace with breathing his last *someday*, he certainly didn't want to rush into eternity on *this* day. Who would protect Mia and Ruthie if he was gone?

Reluctant to admit defeat, he scanned the thick under-growth and tightly packed trees, searching for movement, listening for sound.

Only nature spoke.

Resisting the urge to punch a tree, he looked at Gavin, then turned and trudged toward the house, which was out of sight through the thick wooded area.

They'd walked several steps before Gavin spoke. "It's not your fault, man."

Hayden didn't dignify the comment with a response. Gavin had no idea. Mia and Ruthie were his responsibility, and now, three times, he'd let someone slip past him.

Gavin holstered his sidearm. "I'm the one who lost him. Whoever that was, they clearly know these woods well."

His teammate wasn't the one at fault, but that was a dis-cussion for later. If their runner knew the area, they were likely someone who knew Paige and the Crosbys well.

They could also simply be very comfortable in the out-doors. "Did you get a good look at whoever it was?"

"Jeans. A hoodie. Nothing that stood out. Couldn't even tell you if it was male or female, adult or teen."

No help there. Again. "The person I confronted at the house last night was a man, but the mask and the hood cov-ered too much for me to give a positive ID. I couldn't pick him out of a lineup."

"So basically our suspect pool is—"

"Everyone." They needed more to go on. "I'm not even sure if there's only one attacker or if this is some coordi-nated effort led by…" He waved his hand to indicate the whole planet.

"Why would there be a coordinated effort against a widow and her kid?" Gavin let the question hang as they neared the house, but he stopped walking when their vehicles came into view. "Hayden, aren't you looking into her husband's murder?"

"Yeah." The last thing he wanted to think about was Keith's death. "Why?"

"I'm just throwing out an angle here, something maybe we should consider, but if the SBI is looking into an organized crime link with the shooter, could it be that all of this is somehow connected?"

Hayden stopped so quickly he had to grab a nearby tree for balance. His head spun through Gavin's words, trying to make them translate. "Are you suggesting that Keith's murder wasn't the result of a botched robbery? That he was targeted?"

"I'm just throwing it out there as an angle that was never investigated. That's all."

Who would mark Keith for death? And why? It made no sense.

Although it might explain why the gunman had paced the aisles, seeming to wait for something before he pulled his gun.

Hearing the thought expressed out loud was a gut punch. What if someone had intentionally killed Keith, and now they wanted to harm Mia and Ruthie? How did any of this play into the comment in Watchman's Alley about Mia being a bad mother? "I don't—"

"Hayden McGrath? Is that you?" A voice from the driveway jerked him into the present. They were in an active manhunt, and he needed to pay attention. The past could wait.

He looked in the direction of the person speaking. Eve Warner, Paige's older sister, stood at the edge of the driveway. Her husband, Daniel, walked over from a rugged SUV that was parked in the formerly empty space in the line of cars.

Eve stepped closer. "What are you doing running around

in the woods?" Worried lines wrinkled her forehead. "Is my family okay?"

"Everyone is fine. They're all inside." With all of the trauma of the past twenty-four hours and the new suspicions Gavin's conjecture had ignited, Hayden's brain refused to come up with a creative reason for their jaunt through the trees.

Gavin leaned around him, offering his hand to Eve. "I'm Gavin Mercer, and I work with Hayden at Trinity Investigations. We were just looking around while Mia is inside to see if we could locate any evidence concerning what happened to your sister." He tipped his head. "I'm so sorry for your loss."

Eve's expression drooped as she shook Gavin's hand. "Thank you."

Laying a hand on his wife's shoulder, Daniel clasped Gavin's offered hand. "Thank you. We're all in shock." He gestured toward the house. "Do you want to come inside? When we stepped out, Mia was talking to some friends of the family."

"You were here and you left?" Gavin's voice was even, but it was his investigator voice, one Hayden knew he'd schooled to hide his emotions.

Eve lifted a red-and-green-striped gift bag. "Mia said she and Ruthie are going out of town for Christmas and… Well, here's Ruthie's gift. If she won't be here, I wanted her to have it with her to open on Christmas morning, so I ran home to grab it."

Hayden's heart thawed slightly. The way Mia had included Paige's family in Ruthie's life was rare and beautiful. "I'll put it in the truck, if you'd like."

"Thanks." Eve passed him the bag. "Do you want to come inside and get some coffee or something?"

"We need to get on the road. We've got a long drive ahead

of us." Hopefully, they'd assume Mia was going to her grand-mother's house on the other side of the state. Hayden passed the present to Gavin, who settled it on the truck's hood. "If you'd tell Mia and my friend Rebecca that we're ready to go, I'd appreciate it."

The Warners said their goodbyes and disappeared into the house.

Gavin watched them go. "So those two were unaccounted for when someone was tampering with your ride?" He walked around to the rear of the truck.

Hayden followed. "No motive. There's no reason for them to harm Mia or to question her parenting." He scanned the rear of his pickup, noting the disturbed gravel where their mystery person had knelt.

He squatted and ran his hand beneath the bumper, feeling for a tracking device or an explosive, but nothing was out of place. He shifted his attention to the exhaust. Some-thing had rubbed the interior of the pipe, wiping away accu-mulated dirt and grime. "Gavin." He pointed at the streaks. "Go check your vehicle."

Leaning down, Hayden peered into the tailpipe. Sure enough, a thick rag had been shoved far enough in to avoid easy detection.

Hayden rocked back on his heels as Gavin returned, dan-gling a torn dirt-streaked beach towel from two fingers. "I assume you found something similar?"

He nodded. The method was crude but effective. Block the car's exhaust and the engine would eventually shut down.

Smart play. Incapacitating them would have dropped them helplessly by the side of the road, where they'd be easy tar-gets. He looked up at Gavin, who was watching him with a grim expression.

For the first time, Hayden was truly afraid.

* * *

Mia stared out the kitchen window above Hayden's sink, looking almost directly into the kitchen of the neighbor behind him. While large open spaces made her feel exposed and unprotected, Hayden's relatively new, tightly compacted neighborhood induced a claustrophobia that reminded her of a prison.

Worse, the interior of his house had no warmth. It was artfully designed yet void of personal touches. The builder had painted the walls a beautiful gray set off by white trim, but nothing about the space felt like a home. Hayden had bought furniture from one of those design-your-room-for-you big-box stores. It was all a showroom, made to be looked at but not lived in.

Hayden wasn't image-conscious, but he had no concept of how to decorate, so he'd leaned heavily on the ideas of others. He'd bought the first house he could afford when he took the job with Trinity, putting little thought into anything other than having a place to watch TV and to sleep. Mia had worked hard to keep her mouth shut during the process. It wasn't her business.

The sprawling subdivision featured two-story, four-bedroom homes on quarter-acre lots. There was no view of anything except vinyl siding. While Elizabeth City itself was situated near the mouth of the Pasquotank River where it flowed into the Albemarle Sound, nothing about Hayden's neighborhood spoke of life on the water.

Having been born and raised in Wincombe, living most of her life in view of the Scuppernong River or the Albemarle Sound, Mia had spent her days swimming, paddle boarding and kayaking. Being landlocked wasn't something she was used to. It reminded her of Afghanistan, where there had been no large expanses of water and where danger had lurked around every corner.

Resting her hands on the cool porcelain sink, Mia dropped her chin to her chest. *Lord, I want to go home. I want Ruthie and me to be safe and...* She swallowed icy grief and fear that rushed up her spine. *I want to go back four years to when I felt safe. When I wasn't scared. When I was capable of taking care of my family.*

It felt like centuries had passed. Her life was divided into *before* and *after*. *Before* felt so bright, so safe, so stable. *After* was dark, dangerous and rocky. She'd been a hollow shell of herself for four years.

Maybe the person in Watchman's Alley was right. Maybe Ruthie did deserve a better mother. Even now, Mia was hiding in the kitchen trying to pull herself into some semblance of sanity while Hayden explored the bonus room with Ruthie, where he'd long ago set up a toy land for her visits.

Hayden had been avoiding her since they arrived at his house. Once again, he was hiding something. Everything had been fine at the Crosbys until suddenly, Rebecca had appeared in the living room with Ruthie, subtly herding everyone away from the windows. Likely no one else noticed, but her actions had ignited memories from Mia's time as a deputy and in the military, when slight movements and suggestions shifted people to safety without alarming them.

When they'd set out for Elizabeth City, Hayden had said nothing about a threat. He'd simply driven as fast as legally possible, his eyes shifting constantly between the mirrors and the road. He'd refused to stop, even when Ruthie had complained of hunger. He'd merely reached into the console, passed her a package of peanut butter crackers and trucked on.

They needed to discuss the difference between *protect-*

ing and *lying*. He'd hidden details about Paige's kidnapping from her until it was too late, was keeping something about the attack at her home secret and was up to something when it came to their flight out of town. She was tired of being kept in the—

"Well, Ruthie is excited because the doll she brought with her fits in the new 'take care of your toy baby' set I found online." Hayden's voice, dripping with forced amusement, came from the kitchen door.

Mia straightened and turned, ready to go to battle about the need to know what was happening in her own life. She crossed her arms over her stomach, eyeing the friend she was supposed to trust. "Cut it out, Hay."

He tilted his head, one eyebrow inching toward his hairline. "I'm sorry?"

"I might be dealing with a lot of things, but I'm not made of glass. I won't break." It was a lot easier to be brave when Hayden was standing in front of her and when Rebecca and Gavin were outside watching the perimeter. Their presence gave her the freedom to let go of the fear of physical threats so her emotions could freely breathe. "I want to know everything you aren't telling me."

Hayden stared at her, seeming to gauge how sincere her anger was. Finally, he pulled a stool away from the peninsula that separated the kitchen from the dining room and sat, lacing his fingers on the granite counter. "Somebody tried to make sure our vehicles dumped us on the side of the road on our way out of town. Gavin and I caught them in the act and chased them through the woods, but they got away."

The blunt admission jolted her. Mia reached behind her and grabbed the granite counter. She'd expected him to stall or to deny her accusations, but he'd simply laid everything on the table. It took a second for the shift from expectation to reality to allow understanding. "Someone knew we were at Paige's and tried to sabotage us?"

He nodded, his expression grim. "Either they followed us or..." His gaze slid away from her toward the refrigerator, but he didn't need to say more.

Or they were already at the house and took advantage of the opportunity.

The implications of the unspoken statement weakened Mia's knees. She walked around the counter and sat beside him. Bracing her elbows on the granite, she buried her face in her hands. "So what you're saying is, either you and your team missed a tail or someone in Paige's family is out to get me or Ruthie."

"I'm not saying anything for certain. I'm simply laying out the possibilities." He rested his warm hand between her shoulder blades.

His touch stopped the world from spinning. Hayden was here. His friends were here. Ruthie was safe and she was safe, for the moment at least. In this quiet space, she needed to think like her old self, not the weak, lost, exhausted woman she'd become. "So to figure this out, we need motive as well as opportunity."

"I'm afraid so." Hayden's voice was a low rumble as his thumb swept back and forth along her shoulder blade. "Can we talk about who might have had both of those things this morning?"

His touch soothed the ragged places deep inside of her.

Something in her heart that had felt disjointed since Keith died slipped back into place. For a moment, she felt...whole.

It was unsettling. Sitting up, she effectively dropped Hayden's hand from her back. She placed her palms flat on the counter and forced herself to think through Hayden's question.

She mentally scanned the faces of the mourners and dismissed each one. "Several opportunities but no motives."

"So let's start with opportunity. Walk me through it. Who was out of your sight at any point?"

"The most obvious is Blake Darby."

"Ruthie's bio-dad."

"He was quiet, almost angry. I mean, that's understandable given Paige's death. They were close friends even though they'd broken things off. But he left in a huff a few minutes before Rebecca brought Ruthie inside." She hated to think the young man would harm them, but... "He *is* Ruthie's biological father. Maybe something snapped in him? Maybe he regrets the adoption?" The words sank in rising bile. The idea of someone trying to take her daughter away by any means necessary was—

"Let's remember he willingly signed away his parental rights. He chose to distance himself from Ruthie. He can't go back now, four years later, and rescind that. Don't let an impossibility hang you up. Ruthie is your daughter. Period. Nothing can change that."

Mia drew in a shaky breath. She knew this, but the reassurance was appreciated.

"So, Blake." Stretching across the counter, Hayden grabbed a pad and a pen and started taking notes. "We'll come back to possible motives later. Focus on opportunity now."

Smart man. Conjecturing about motives would spiral her imagination out of control. Facts would keep her steady. "Okay. Paige's dad was supposedly up in her room, but I never saw him." She picked at a hangnail on her thumb. "He was never happy about the adoption so—"

"No motives. Just opportunity." Hayden wrote *Cade Crosby* on his list. "Who else?"

"I hate to say it, but Sue followed Blake out." There was no way Paige's mother was behind any of this, though.

"We have to consider every angle." Hayden made the note. "Anyone else?" He looked up. "Wait. Daniel and Eve pulled up after we chased the man into the woods. They said they'd run home to grab Ruthie's Christmas present."

Mia nodded. "Yes, but I can't imagine a reason they'd—"

"Every angle."

As long as they were conjecturing, there was one thing that bothered her. "Paige's mentor, Amanda Rhinehart, and her husband, Trent, were there. They didn't leave, but he gave me an odd feeling."

Hayden's pencil paused over the page. "How so?"

"I can't really explain it. It was something about the way—"

"Mommy!" Ruthie burst into the kitchen, a doll strapped into a miniature purple carrier on her chest. "I'm hungry! Can we get nuggets?"

Mia jumped and laid her hand on her chest. "Ruthie. Inside voice. Please."

Skidding to a halt next to Mia, Ruthie planted her fists on her hips and tilted her head. "Penelope and I want nuggets. Please."

At least her voice was a little softer on this go-round. They could work on requests in the form of questions instead of demands later.

Mia looked over her shoulder at Hayden, who mouthed, *Penelope?* He turned the notepad face down on the counter as though Ruthie could read cursive.

Then again, when it came to her daughter, who knew what deeper talents she was hiding. She was a smart one.

Mia took a deep breath, pulled herself into the moment and smiled down into her daughter's hazel eyes as she answered Hayden's question. "*Somebody* has watched a lot of

Wreck-It Ralph. And *somebody* wanted to be just like Vanellope von Schweetz, but *somebody* had an easier time with their *p*'s than their *v*'s."

"And I like Penelope better." Ruthie bent at the waist to lean closer, her fists still on her hips. "Nuggets, *please*."

It was obvious from the bossiness that Ruthie was pushed to the edge of her four-year-old limits. As much as Mia didn't indulge her daughter's every whim, it was still wise to tread lightly when food and a nap were needed. "Let's do that tomorrow. It's Sunday, and we can't go get the chicken nuggets that are your favorites. I'm sure—"

"It's *Sunday*?" Ruthie's voice screeched to nuclear octaves. She stepped back as though Mia had personally insulted her. "My Christmas play! We can't stay at Uncle Hayden's. We have to go now. It's tonight!" She grabbed Mia's wrist and tugged.

Hayden grabbed the back of Mia's shirt to keep her from toppling to the floor.

The Christmas play. The children's reenactment of the Christmas story was a Sunday-night-before-Christmas tradition. It had been the topic of discussion in their house morning, noon and night for weeks. Anyone listening would think Ruthie's small speaking role had her Tony-Awards bound.

As tears welled in her daughter's eyes, Mia dug her teeth into her lip. How could she explain to a four-year-old that the event she'd looked forward to the most might just get them killed?

EIGHT

Hayden's heart broke for his goddaughter. She'd recited her line, "Look at all of the shiny angels," complete with a dramatic flourish toward the sky, at least a hundred times on their outing the morning before. He'd heard it at least a thousand more during her pre-bedtime energy surge the night before.

In their rush to safety, the adults had forgotten the importance of a little girl's Christmas excitement. This would crush Ruthie.

He had to fix it.

Mia tugged her sweater from Hayden's grip, then slipped down to kneel in front of her daughter.

Right. Hayden sat against the stool's back and braced his hands on his thighs. This wasn't his to fix, but he'd do anything to dry the tears already pooling in those precious little eyes.

"Baby, I know this isn't going to make a lot of sense to you, but I need you to listen." Mia laid her hands on her daughter's shoulders. "Sometimes we look forward to things for a really long time. We dream about them, and we plan them, and we look forward to them. They're wonderful and important, and we're really excited about them, just like you've been so excited about the play tonight."

Ruthie tried to pull away, angling for the arched opening that led into the living room. "So we have to go. This is wonderful and important, and we're going to *miss* it."

Hayden wrestled a rush of emotion. He looked down at his hands, running his thumb over a fresh cut on his wrist, probably from his dash through the woods earlier.

Mia's words resonated. Sometimes dreams and plans fell apart. That truth wasn't fair to Ruthie today. It wasn't fair to Mia four years ago. It wasn't fair to him when Beth walked away. *Sometimes, God, life just seems mean.*

Gently, Mia turned her daughter to face her. "Ruthie, I need you to hear me. Can you look in my eyes and listen?"

Ruthie huffed and crossed her arms over her baby doll, eyeing her mother with suspicion.

Mia laid her hand on the baby's head. "You love Penelope, right?"

Like a real mother, Ruthie's expression softened. "Yes." She tucked her chin tightly to her chest and kissed the doll's head.

"And you'd do anything to keep her safe, right?"

"I won't let anything happen to her. I promise."

"I know that, and Penelope knows that. What you need to know is that's how Mommy feels about you. And that's also how God feels about me and you and Uncle Hayden. We all want the people we love to be safe, right?"

Ruthie's eyes narrowed as though she was beginning to understand that there would be no Christmas play.

"Well, sweetie, there are some grown-up things happening right now, so the grown-ups have to keep everybody safe. One of the things we have to do is stay at Uncle Hayden's for a few days."

"Like a sleepover? Like when we went to Noni's during the hurry-cane?"

"Just like that."

Hayden nodded, impressed at Ruthie's understanding. Back in September, Mia had packed up Ruthie, then Hayden had driven them across the state to her grandmother's house as a precaution when Hurricane Jessica threatened to hit the area. The storm had turned eastward at the last second, dampening its effects on the coast, but this was the perfect way for Ruthie to relate to what was happening.

For a moment, it seemed Ruthie accepted the situation, but she suddenly stood taller. "So we're going back for the play. Right now. Because there isn't a hurry-cane."

"Baby, no. This time is different. It's not a—"

"My play!" Ruthie stomped her foot, a full-blown tantrum raining like the hurricane under discussion. "I tell about the angels. Somebody has to tell about the angels. It's important!" Her voice rose to window-rattling levels. "I have to go!"

Mia's posture mimicked her daughter's, spine straight and expression brooking no more discussion. "Ruthie, I'm sorry. I really am. But you can't yell at adults. I know this is making you sad and angry, and I hate that more than anything. Do you need a hug or do you need a few minutes in the playroom by yourself?"

Ruthie's face was stormy. "By myself." She practically shouted her decision, then turned and flounced from the room.

No teenager had ever strutted in such a dismissive manner. Hayden wasn't sure whether to be impressed or terrified as Ruthie thumped up the stairs with the foot-stomping force of an elephant.

Both he and Mia jumped when the door to the bonus room slammed.

With a loud exhale, Mia dropped back onto her heels. Her head bent forward.

Hayden's already broken heart shattered. Ruthie's pain was Mia's pain, and all of it was his pain.

He slid off the stool and sat on the floor, facing her. "I'm sorry."

"It's not your fault." Mia swiped at a tear that ran down her cheek. "It's just not fair."

"No, it's not." He warred between sorrow and anger, his heartache for those he cared about clashing swords with fury at the person who had made this flight necessary. He wanted to hold Mia and Ruthie close and to dry their tears, but, at the same time, he wanted to storm out the door and hunt down the villain behind this.

He'd never felt so torn in his life.

Mia sniffed, cooling some of his ire. At the moment, he couldn't fight the forces outside, but he could do something about the storm raging under his roof.

He watched Mia swipe away another tear. Recent…feelings…said he should be careful about touching her, but he couldn't let her drown in anguish while he simply sat and waited for it all to somehow get better. He'd comforted her many times in the past, so why should now be any different?

It could *not* be any different. He had to maintain their friendship, because if things changed between them…

Shaking off the thought, he rested his hand on her shoulder. "This won't last forever. Nothing ever does."

Mia sniffed. "Good or bad, it all ends, doesn't it?"

She wasn't just talking about Ruthie's tantrum or their present danger.

"What did you just tell Ruthie?" Her words to her daughter worked their way from his head into his heart. "That God loves us and wants us to be safe? He has our best in mind, just like mommies and daddies do for their kids? That applies to you, too."

Her head jerked toward him, and she stared at him through narrowed eyes. It was tough to say if she was angry or thinking. After several heartbeats, she swiped her face and twisted her lips to the side. "Keith and Paige both being murdered is way bigger than a missed Christmas play."

"Not to be disrespectful or to dismiss the severity of what's happened but, in this moment, that Christmas play means the world to Ruthie."

"Four-year-olds don't see the world the same way adults do, especially when they've been sheltered from the truth." Mia shook her head and turned her attention to her fingers, which were knit in her lap. "Thanks for the reminder. You're going to be a great dad someday."

The sentiment drove straight into his heart, skipping the beats out of rhythm. There were a lot of things he could say about that statement, from sappy to serious to way out of line. He chose a fourth option. The moment could use a little levity. "Hey, I'm already the greatest godfather that ever existed."

Mia sniffed and laughed. "You sound like you're about to make me an offer I can't refuse." She quoted one of the most famous lines ever uttered in a movie, tilting her head to meet his gaze with a spark of humor in her eye.

But a different implication to the words zipped through Hayden. What if he offered her his future?

Mia must have seen the shock his own thought rattled through him, because her expression shifted, her smile melting into something Hayden couldn't read. Something that might be surprise or even fear.

He needed to backpedal fast. This thing that had churned up inside of him over the past twenty-four hours was just a side effect of overwrought emotions. It would pass.

He forced a smile. "Actually, I don't have an offer, but I do have an idea to help Ruthie cope with the disappointment." It was risky, but the risks could be mitigated. If it helped the little girl, who had wrapped him around her little finger from the moment she was born, to cope with the chaos swirling around her, then he'd find a way to make it happen.

Tilting her head, Mia regarded him almost as though she knew he was running away from something in his heart. She didn't call him on it, though. She merely stood and brushed off her jeans. "I'm good with anything that will help her. Within reason, of course. This whole situation is so unfair to her."

Hayden scrambled to his feet. "It is. I can't offer her the dream role of Heralding Shepherd in a play, but I can provide a relatively safe substitute."

"Go on."

"There's a farm about twenty minutes from here. They do this huge, multi-acre drive-through Christmas light display. We don't even have to get out of the car to see it. It starts just after sunset and, if we get there when the gates open, we won't have to deal with as many people. I promise she'll be wowed by it." His church small group had volunteered in the prayer tent and had made the drive the previous year, and even the adults had been impressed.

Mia leaned against the counter and stared out the window above the sink, chewing her thumbnail. There was no way she realized she was doing it or she'd have already stopped.

Hayden refrained from reaching over to pull her hand from her mouth, although she'd often told him to do that. It would only distract her from the risk assessment she was running in her head.

She lowered her hand. "Rebecca and Gavin would trail us?"

"I'm thinking they'd love to see the lights themselves, so

most definitely." He hoped. He'd certainly call in a ton of favors to get them to do so. And if not them, Kelsie McIlheney and Elliott had offered to step in to add an extra level of security if needed. "I don't think whoever was coming at you realizes we've relocated here. Unless they know you really well and know where I live, I doubt they'll find us." It wasn't totally without risk, but Ruthie needed something, and they couldn't let fear hem them in.

Mia nodded, though the tight lines around her mouth indicated she did so with reservations. "Okay. Hopefully this will help her out."

And hopefully, his soft heart for his goddaughter wasn't about to drive them straight into danger.

"Mommy! Look!" How Ruthie's squeal hadn't already broken the windshield of Hayden's pickup was beyond Mia's ability to comprehend. Her ears were still ringing from the last eight excited outbursts.

Hayden chuckled, though he kept his attention on the car in front of them. They snaked along in a line of cars that wound through trees and fields filled with too many Christmas lights and displays to count. He had tuned the radio to the instructed station at the beginning of the twenty-minute drive, and the familiar litany of the Grinch's many faults graveled from the speakers. Despite his belief that they'd beat the crowds by coming early, they were far from the first car in line.

Trying to shake out the discomfort in her ears, Mia swallowed the automatic *Inside voice, please* that wanted to rise up. Her daughter needed the freedom to be an awestruck child tonight.

They all needed to be awestruck children tonight.

She looked to where Ruthie was strapped into her booster in the back seat. "What do you want me to see?"

Ruthie waved excitedly toward the windshield. "It's the Grinch and Max! And they're zooming down the mountain!" She swooshed her hand to illustrate their journey.

Hayden tapped Mia's knee and pointed to the left. Sure enough, on a small hill that sloped down to the wide path they were on, a Grinch made entirely out of lights guided his sleigh toward them. His long-suffering dog, Max, galloped in the lead thanks to the magic of multiple flashing lights.

Mia laughed. The Grinch was Ruthie's favorite, and his story was interspersed with the various other displays throughout the show.

As Ruthie giggled, Mia glanced into the side mirror, where the headlights from Rebecca and Gavin's sedan followed close behind.

The song on the radio faded and shifted to the Chipmunks singing about their two front teeth as a lit display of the animals appeared in front of them.

Mia allowed herself to relax and take in the Christmas cheer. For the moment, they were safe. Ensconced in the pickup with the heater blasting and the cheerful music playing, she could almost pretend that the world was as it should be.

Almost. Outside of the relative safety of the winding drive and the hundreds of other cars in front of and behind them, danger lurked.

But what had her therapist said to her so many times? *Be in the moment you're in. Not in the past. Not in the future. Enjoy the now.*

The *now* was pretty close to, well, *normal.*

Ruthie squealed again.

The *now* was also pretty loud.

Pressing her palm to her ear, she looked at Ruthie and laughed as her daughter bounced in her seat. It was a good thing the cup of hot chocolate Hayden had purchased through the window as they'd pulled up to the gates had a lid on it. Otherwise, the interior of Hayden's truck would never be the same.

Ruthie didn't offer an explanation for her excitement this time. She simply looked from right to left, trying to take it all in. The lights reflected in her eyes, filling them with wonder.

For the first time in four years, wrapped in the safety of Hayden's truck, Mia felt fear release, allowing in a peace she'd chased for what felt like an eternity.

As she started to turn back to the front, she caught Hayden's gaze. In the brief moment that their eyes locked, electricity zipped between them, arcing down her spine from the top of her head to the tips of her toes.

What was *that*?

She whipped to the front, pressing her back into the seat and her toes into the floor. An electric tingle chased the zap down her spine until her nervous system finally righted itself.

Gratitude. That's all it was. Hayden was always here, always taking care of her and of Ruthie. He was a constant in their lives, and he sacrificed so much more than she would ever dare to ask of him. It was as simple as that.

"You okay?" Hayden's voice barely drifted over the Chipmunks' song. It was the first time he'd spoken since they'd followed the car in front of them onto the path of Christmas cheer.

"Fine." She'd better get herself back to normal quickly. Hayden was perceptive, and that little *zap* could definitely put the awkward into their friendship if he picked up on it. "I'm just…content. At least for right now." She dared to squeeze his wrist where his hand rested on the gearshift.

"Thank you. This was so much more than I thought it would be, and I think I needed it even more than Ruthie did."

When she gathered herself enough to look up, his gaze darted between hers and the slow-moving car in front of them. "I'm glad." He slipped his hand from the gearshift and entwined his fingers with hers, offering a quick squeeze.

Mia squeezed back, but when she tried to pull away, Hayden didn't let go.

The warmth of his touch, the solidness of his presence, the oasis of calm inside the vehicle… It all washed a peace through her that she hadn't experienced in years. A feeling of being in the right place with the right person.

Digging her teeth into her lower lip, Mia gently untangled her fingers from his and pulled her hand into her lap. She was only feeling safe because Hayden was her friend and was a constant in her life. She couldn't sink any deeper into this than friendship. There could never be anything past that. Hayden deserved more than to be shackled to a broken single mother whom he'd have to take care of for the rest of his days.

He deserved someone…normal.

With a sigh, she looked out the side window, desperate for a distraction. "Ruthie, look." She pointed into the woods at the edge of a large field. "There's Snoopy."

Ruthie clapped her hands as the song on the radio changed to the tale of Snoopy and the Red Baron. It was a thing of wonder how technology could so seamlessly line everything up into a precise, dependable experience.

If only life worked that way.

As they wound toward the end of the drive, the music shifted to traditional Christmas hymns, and the lit displays featured the story of Jesus's birth, from Mary on a donkey with Joseph leading the way to a chorus of glowing angels suspended from the trees above a group of gaping shepherds.

"Hey, Mommy!" Ruthie leaned forward as far as she could, pointing to the angels. "Look at all of the shiny angels!" She recited the line she should have been speaking at the church at almost this exact moment, had things been as they should. Rather than disappointment, though, she sounded excited and happy, and she joined in with the radio to sing "Away in a Manger" as they passed the Nativity scene that was the last display on the drive.

Her daughter's joy was thanks to Hayden and his quick thinking.

She started to tell him so, but Ruthie's voice shattered her thoughts. "Mommy! Uncle Hayden! Look!"

Hayden muttered under his breath. In the dim light, he winced and mouthed, *I forgot.*

As Ruthie bounced in her seat, Mia looked out the windshield. Across a large grassy parking lot, a painted plywood Christmas village that included several small stores and a café shone through the darkness. To the right, a large open gazebo featured a live Santa and Mrs. Claus, visiting with children who raced toward them.

Oh, no. Every ounce of cheer drained out of Mia. Ruthie would melt down if they bypassed the scene to follow the exit signs onto the road.

But they didn't dare stop and join the crowds making their way between the shops and the Santa display. There were too many people. It was too risky. The crowds were more than Mia was prepared to handle, and there was no way for Hayden and his friends to ensure they'd be safe if they exited his truck.

Her peace shattered, and the shards sliced into her lungs, making it hard to breathe. Everything she knew about being a mother said her child pitching a hissy fit wasn't the end of the world. Piled onto everything else, though, it felt like more than either of them could handle.

Hayden slowed, increasing the space between his truck and the car in front of them. "Ruthie, let's make a deal."

The excited chatter stopped, followed by a suspicious, "What kind of deal?"

The child was savvy. She knew a *deal* meant she wasn't going to get what she wanted.

Hayden tapped Mia on the knee. When she looked up, he whispered, "Trust me?" His arched eyebrow spoke of uncertainty.

Mia nodded. He knew she did.

With an answering tip of his head, he proceeded in an overly cheerful voice. "The line for Santa is really long. How about instead of freezing our toes and fingers off waiting to see him, we go back to my house and watch the Grinch movie instead."

"But, Santa!" The whine was in full effect.

"I wasn't finished." Hayden upped the cheer another notch.

"Okay." Ruthie's reply was dubious.

"I'll take you through the drive-through at the ice cream place and you can have whatever you want."

"Even sprinkles?"

Mia slumped in her seat. It seemed the crisis was averted. While she wouldn't typically approve of bribing her daughter out of a tantrum, extenuating circumstances ruled the day.

"Triple sprinkles." Hayden agreed to the terms of surrender.

"Yay! Let's go!" Ruthie's cheer was restored, but her voice quickly changed. "Mommy?"

Mia squeezed her eyes shut. She knew that tone. What was coming would be tough to wriggle out of, especially since they were twenty minutes from any sort of civilization besides the light show. "Yes, baby?"

"I have to go potty."

Air hissed between Hayden's teeth. Yeah, even he knew this was going to be difficult. He followed a path, parking the truck at the end of a long row of vehicles. "Our church worked out here one year, staffing the prayer tent they have by the Santa display. There's a smaller separate set of bathrooms used by volunteers that the public doesn't know about." He looked at her. "There might be a couple of volunteers who come in and out because there are two stalls, but it'll keep you out of the crowds."

She could handle that.

As Rebecca pulled up beside them, Hayden walked around the truck to tell her and Gavin what was going on.

Ruthie started the little dance that let Mia know she wasn't going to make it much longer.

No one was around the small plywood building Hayden had indicated, tucked away several feet from the end of the row of shops. Hayden could see her from where he stood.

Tugging Ruthie's hand, they headed for the restroom, and Mia waited by the sinks for Ruthie to take care of herself. After Ruthie washed her hands, she wandered to the open doorway while Mia washed hers, keeping one eye on her daughter.

Ruthie leaned out the door. "Hello!"

Mia's heart picked up speed. Ruthie had never met a stranger she wouldn't talk to, but now was not the time for her to be making new friends. She quickly shook off her hands as Ruthie stepped closer to the door.

A low voice spoke outside, and Ruthie nodded. "The lights were so pretty, and I saw the Grinch so many times!"

The voice spoke again, and Ruthie took another step toward the door.

Mia practically leaped for her daughter. "Time to go, Ruthie." She latched on to Ruthie's shoulder as a person kneeling in the shadows to the side of the door stood and backed away.

A familiar person.

Reflexively, Mia jerked Ruthie up into her arms and screamed for Hayden.

NINE

Hayden sprinted toward the small huts with Mia's scream echoing in his ears. He'd had the restrooms within his sight the entire time. What had happened?

Two car doors slammed. Rebecca and Gavin were right behind him.

Mia was backing into the open door of the bathroom, holding Ruthie tightly against her.

A figure darted into the shadows, running into the space between buildings and disappearing into the darkness behind the row of shops.

Hayden yelled orders over his shoulder. "Rebecca. Gavin. Behind the building!"

"Saw them." Rebecca acknowledged the command, veering in that direction with Gavin at her heels. They were more than capable of handling the threat that was, fortunately, heading away from the holiday revelers in the Christmas village.

It took him what seemed like years to reach Mia and Ruthie. By the time he got to the wooden steps of the small building, his heart was pounding as though he didn't run five miles most mornings.

Mia's face was pale, even in the dim light filtering out from the restrooms.

Ruthie's eyes were wide with shock. Her young mind was likely incapable of processing anything that had happened.

Hayden pulled them close, with Ruthie sandwiched between him and Mia. Mia began to tremble so hard that Hayden could hear her teeth knocking together. "What happened?"

Ruthie wriggled and squirmed until Hayden was forced to back away so Mia could set her down. He looked at Ruthie, who stood in the gap between them, her fists pressed into her hips in a familiar exasperated gesture.

She glared up at Hayden. "I was talking to a nice lady, and Mommy yelled and scared me."

Hayden's gaze rose to Mia's. Had she panicked at the sight of one of the volunteers and frightened an innocent woman into the woods?

No. The fear in Mia's expression was different. This wasn't like the moments when her emotions took over her rational thinking. Her wide eyes were clear and terrified.

She kept her hands firmly planted on her daughter's shoulders. Her lips parted as though she might speak, but then she looked down at Ruthie. She stared at her little girl for a long time before she lifted her head and shook it once, tight-lipped. Whatever she needed to say, she wasn't going to risk frightening her daughter any more than she already had. "We should go."

They should. Getting the two of them to safety was Hayden's first priority. When he had the whole story, he might need to call the sheriff and Ross Hartnett, who owned the farm hosting the light show, to alert them if the threat turned out to be credible.

He was reluctant to leave without Rebecca and Gavin. His team would provide protection from the rear, watching for a tail as they headed back to his house. Although he had no idea what had scared Mia, the fear that they'd been found dominated his thoughts.

With one arm protectively around Mia and the other hand on Ruthie's shoulder, he turned them toward the parking lot. He'd get them into the truck and—

"McGrath," Gavin called out as he jogged up with Rebecca. His grim expression confirmed the worst. "Whoever it was, they had a head start. This place backs up to a pretty dense wooded area. They could be anywhere or they could be long gone, but we're both pretty sure it was a female."

"Police?" Hayden reached for his phone.

"No." Mia was emphatic. "Technically, there's no crime, and we don't dare risk crying wolf."

She was right. There was no crime to report…yet.

Hayden herded everyone toward the truck, debating whether or not to make the call. Caution said he should, but raising a false alarm could slow the response if they really needed help in the future.

Fine. Until he got the whole story, they were on their own. Hayden kept walking as Gavin took up a position beside him and Rebecca moved around to walk with Mia.

Hayden took charge. "Follow us back to the house. Watch for a tail." He kept his voice low to prevent Ruthie from hearing. If she found out that her drive-through ice cream had been taken off the table, it might be one disappointment too many. While she was normally a well-behaved kid, the chaos around her had drawn out a rare irritability. It was better to deal with the emotional fallout at home.

He would have someone run to the store and buy every sprinkle on the ice cream aisle if he had to, but that wasn't his number-one priority.

Right now, he had to get his girls to safety and find out what had happened.

He ushered them into the truck and handed his phone back to Ruthie to distract her. They were on the road and moving along the miles-long line of cars that waited for admittance into the light show before he spoke. Glancing in the rearview to ensure Ruthie was sufficiently occupied and his trail vehicle was in place, he kept his voice low. "What happened?" It wasn't like Mia to scream.

Mia balled her fists on her knees and turned from where she'd been staring out the side window. Lines creased her forehead and dug trenches beside her mouth.

He'd seen this posture before. She was fighting a panic attack.

Times like this made him feel helpless. Sometimes she wanted to be comforted, but other times she wanted to be left alone as she went to war with her own mind and body. He never knew what to do until he tried.

Reaching across the console, he took a chance that she'd prefer to be comforted. He laid his hand on her clenched fist. "I'm here. Gavin and Rebecca are right behind us. You're safe right now. Let me handle the details. It's okay to let go."

Impossibly, her muscles tightened. One hand darted for the door, and she laid a finger on the button to roll down the window, seeking fresh air.

As suddenly as she'd tensed, her body relaxed. Her right hand fell to the seat beside her, and her fist relaxed beneath his grip. In the headlights of the vehicles lined up beside the road, tears glistened down her cheeks. "I'm not losing my mind."

"Nobody said you were." Was she doubting what she'd seen? Had she panicked and misread the situation?

He didn't want to think so. Even in the depths of fear, Mia managed to maintain a semblance of situational awareness. The things in her mind tended to frighten her more than the dangers she encountered in real life. "Can you tell me what happened?"

She relayed a stop-and-start story about Ruthie talking to someone at the door, but then she grew quiet. When she looked at Hayden, determination had set her jaw and had erased the lines that fear had etched into her forehead. "The woman Ruthie was talking to? I've seen her before." Mia leaned closer and lowered her voice. "Yesterday, at the café. She's the one with the backpack."

"The one who looked familiar to you?" This couldn't be a coincidence. Mia crossing paths with the same random woman twice in two different towns in two days was definitely odd. "You're certain?"

"Yes, Hayden." Her voice cracked like a whip. "I'm not losing my mind."

He winced, then reset his expression. Fear often lit a fire under Mia's anger. Volcanic emotions tended to erupt with various forms of lava. Sometimes it was hard not to take offense. It took restraint not to react, to step back and respond with kindness when he came under friendly fire.

Hayden kneaded the steering wheel as they reached the last in the long line of cars. He eyed the dark two-lane road ahead of them, where danger could be lurking.

In the rearview, Gavin's sedan kept pace about four car lengths back, standing between them and any threats from the rear. Several other vehicles followed them, likely other spectators who were making their way back to the four-lane state highway. Once there, it would be easier to determine if they had picked up a tail. He'd drive the exact speed limit, and most cars would pass them. After that, he'd take the most winding way home possible.

With Rebecca and Gavin watching the rear, Hayden could focus on Mia. He'd never been more grateful for his team.

Their vigilance gave him time to pull away from the unfamiliar role of bodyguard into the more comfortable roles of friend and investigator.

If this woman had been able to flush Mia out of the restaurant in Wincombe and had also managed to find them near Elizabeth City, then... "I think we need to look at the possibility that the person who attacked you in Watchman's Alley might have been this woman."

Mia lifted her chin, staring at the ceiling of the pickup. "I've considered that. But did she purposely come into the café to unsettle me, knowing that I have panic attacks and she'd throw me off balance enough to make me run? Or did she randomly walk in, see me, then take her chances when I went into the alley? While a lot of people know what I'm going through emotionally, not a lot of people would know how to..." Her voice dropped. "How to pull my strings like I'm a puppet."

"Hey." He took her hand, needing to comfort her but also needing to watch the dark road ahead of them. "None of this is your fault."

Mia turned away. She pulled her hand from his, withdrawing into herself.

Hayden glanced at Ruthie in the rearview to make sure she was still engrossed in his phone, then turned his attention to the windshield. While the danger outside was very real, the bigger threat might be to Mia's mental health. If these attacks kept coming, she might turn completely inside to protect herself.

And that could be the most dangerous thing of all.

Mia sank onto Hayden's leather sofa and pulled a cream-colored throw pillow onto her lap, staring at the blank television screen above his fireplace.

The house was silent. *Finally.* Pumped full of holiday cheer, the Grinch cartoon and ice cream sprinkles provided by Hayden's boss, Ruthie hadn't settled down until nearly ten. Hayden had carried her up to the guest room, then disappeared while Mia had prepared her limp and exhausted daughter for bed. Ruthie had dropped off the moment her head hit the pillow.

Mia's ears were tired. Her body was tired. Her emotions were tired. All she wanted was to run until she couldn't run any more, until she finally felt safe.

At the moment, it seemed nowhere would ever feel safe again. Not her hometown. Not her home. Not Hayden's house. The places she'd always counted on were all compromised.

Hayden's alarm keypad sounded a two-tone chime, and the door that led to the garage closed softly. A low rumble indicated that Hayden had pushed the button to lower the exterior garage door. Several beeps drifted from the kitchen as he set the alarm for the night.

Would it do any good? Her home had an alarm, but that hadn't stopped someone from trying to smoke them out.

When he walked through the kitchen doorway, he didn't seem surprised to see her on the couch. He looked slightly sheepish. "Sorry about Ruthie bouncing off the walls tonight. The sugar rush was totally my fault."

She actually smiled. "Yeah, I'm pretty sure her mother never authorized feeding her an entire container of ice cream sprinkles, but hey, you're here to deal with the consequences so I'm passing the torch." If Ruthie woke up crying with a stomachache, she'd gladly tell Hayden *I told you so.* "Still, it was worth it to see her happy. I think you might have successfully overwritten the memory of her mom freaking out at the bathroom door because she was talking to a 'nice lady.'" The words tasted bitter. While the grown-ups had to worry about threats, her daughter was still free to view life through a child's eyes. It was a blessing and a curse as Mia tried to teach her daughter to navigate a world that would gladly eat them both alive. The trick was guiding her toward wisdom while maintaining Ruthie's innocence.

And now that the hypothetical threats were real?

Mia drew her finger along the edge of the pillow. "I don't know how to handle any of this." She looked up at Hayden, who hadn't moved from the doorway. "Whoever thinks their husband is going to be murdered? That four years later, someone will try to hurt them as well? This doesn't happen in real life, does it?"

"You were a soldier and a law enforcement officer." He walked over and sat on the other end of the couch, angling toward her. "You know the answer to that question."

It did happen. Every day. But it happened to other people, not to her. "This can't be my life. It's just not…real."

"You've told me before that anxiety makes you feel like you've taken a step back from reality. Maybe—"

Mia rocketed to her feet, the pillow dropping to the floor. "Why can't I shake this? Why does everything go back to the night Keith died? Why can't I just be…?" She threw her hands into the air, the words refusing to form. Since that awful night, nothing had been the same. The thing that had changed the most was the monster that lived inside of her mind, spinning frightening tall tales. It was never silent, at least not for long. It was always telling her that danger lurked around every corner, that something bad could happen to her or to Ruthie at any moment. Worse, it often told her exactly what that person had hissed hot against her ear in the alley.

That she was a terrible mother.

She wrapped her arms around her stomach and turned

away from Hayden, looking up at the ceiling fan. It could use a good dusting.

Why was she noticing that now?

"I'm not losing my mind." Was she? Because the threat wasn't just being whispered into her brain this time. It was truly all around her.

Unless she was imagining everything.

The couch rustled behind her, then Hayden was there. He laid his hands on her shoulders and rested his chin on top of her head. "That's the third time you've said that tonight."

"Said what?" She wanted to step away, but she couldn't. The firm pressure of his hands on her shoulders and the warmth of his presence so close behind held her captive, but not in a bad way. It hemmed her in. Made her feel safe. Made her feel like maybe she wasn't about to drown beneath a wave of panic.

His chest moved against her back as he spoke. "You're not losing your mind. Nobody thinks you are, least of all me." He gently turned her to face him, then reset his hands on her shoulders. "Mia, I know the hardest part of this isn't the fear itself, the things digging into your thoughts. It's the ripple effect. You think people look at you differently. It's damaged your entire life. You think you're weak, but in re- ality, you're probably the strongest person I've ever known."

Mia shook her head. He had no idea what she endured every single day.

"No, ma'am." His voice was gentle as he stepped around in front of her. He tipped his head to try to catch her eye, but she focused on the knit of his blue sweater where it stretched across his chest. "Don't do this to yourself. A grenade got tossed into the center of your world, and the damage was im- mense. Some of it can't be repaired. Keith can't come back to life. Think about it like combat. Explosions cause concussive injuries. Some are temporary, others are permanent, but none are the injured person's fault. They didn't pull the pin." He hooked his finger under her chin and forced her to meet his eye. "Just like soldiers have to do hard work to heal from physical injuries, it takes hard work to come back from mental and emotional ones. You're building something new, something that won't look like the old way. You're recovering. That takes time and energy and strength, and I admire you for it. I wish…" His gaze slid from hers, lingering on something to his right.

Mia's mouth went dry. Something was…shifting. It was in the feel of his hands on her shoulders. The deep rumble of his words. The look in his eye. It reached into places in her heart that had long been parched and dead, and rained new life.

Hayden was her friend. Her confidant. But could there be something more? Because right now, more than she'd ever wanted anything in her life, she wanted to close the distance between them. She wanted to feel the full circle of his arms around her, knowing if he held her close that she'd be warm and safe and…

Whole.

Her lungs couldn't take in a full breath, but, far from the panic attacks that usually robbed her of air, this was different. This was something she hadn't felt since…since forever. Something that made her want to connect to this man in a way she'd never thought she would want to connect with anyone again.

Hayden's gaze returned to hers and lingered, searching. The longer he searched, the more she wanted to stay here forever. The more his expression softened, the more he looked like he wanted to—

His eyes dropped to her lips, then slowly scanned her face before returning, asking for permission.

Mia's heart kicked up to a dangerous pace. He had to be able to feel it.

But she didn't look away. Hopefully, he'd understand that—

His hands slid along her shoulders and up her neck, cupping her jaw. His thumbs stroked her cheeks. He leaned closer, raising her head slightly, and brushed her lips softly, returning to deepen the kiss before she could catch her breath.

Pulling her closer, his touch shattered her fear, reminding her what it felt like to be safe and sheltered and whole.

TEN

Hayden's knees went weak. He was pretty sure it was Mia holding the two of them up, because it certainly wasn't him. No woman had ever literally stolen his strength before. Not even when he'd been engaged to Beth had he felt his entire core so rattled, so—

Beth. Keith.

Mia.

Hayden inhaled sharply and backed away, his arms up and out to the sides as though he wanted to prove he was unarmed. "Mia, I am so sorry." He never should have kissed her. Never should have let himself get so caught up in a moment of admiration that he crossed a line.

She was his best friend. She was his best friend's wife. She was—

His head spun. But Keith was gone. Mia was a widow.

What was right? What was…what was anything? Mia talked so often about feeling detached from reality. He definitely felt like his life was not his own right now, as though he was watching it on a television screen.

Mia stumbled backward, her eyes wide. "I…" She pointed vaguely toward the stairs. "I have to go. Ruthie… I need…" Shaking her head, her expression a mixture of confusion and pain, she practically ran up the stairs without looking back.

Hayden's heart fell as he watched her retreat. Yeah, he'd crossed a line. A big one. Worse, he couldn't even explain why. Sure, he'd been feeling...things...for the past day or so, but he hadn't realized...

Forget it. He scooped the discarded throw pillow from the floor, a "decorating touch" his mother had chosen, and sat heavily on the couch, letting the pillow drop onto his lap. His head fell to the back cushions. He wrapped his forearms over his face. He was an idiot, plain and simple. What kind of guy kissed his best friend, especially when her life was in so much turmoil that she'd confessed she had no idea which way was up?

Needing to move, he flung the pillow to the side and stalked to the back door in the kitchen. He turned off the alarm, hoping the chimes wouldn't frighten Mia, then stepped onto the patio, where two canvas beach chairs were the only furnishings. He dropped into one and turned his face to the stars, but no prayers would come.

He was an awful person. He'd failed to protect Mia and instead had selfishly taken advantage of both of their emotional upheaval. For what?

For a kiss.

A kiss that had been life-changing. Literally breathtaking. That had—

"You look like a man who regrets every single one of his life decisions."

At the deep voice from his left, Hayden jumped up and whirled, ready to fight.

It was Elliott, who'd switched places with Gavin for the night. His boss walked to the chair next to Hayden and sat, stretching his legs in front of him and crossing his ankles as though they were two buddies chatting after a cookout.

What would it be like to be as confident as Elliott? He

was unflappable, always analyzing, never "up in his feels," as he'd heard some of the younger members at church say. As much as Hayden hated that phrase, he definitely understood what it meant tonight.

"McGrath? You asleep over there?" Elliott's voice held the thread of sarcastic amusement that marked his personality.

"Deciding how much I want to say." He'd always been able to talk to his boss and friend, but this felt sort of like a high-school-crush problem and not an adult issue that needed to be analyzed.

"Hmm." Lacing his hands on his stomach, Elliott stared at the privacy fence at the back of the small yard. "I'm going to guess this is about more than figuring out who's hunting Mia and whether or not they've found you guys here." Without lifting his head from the back of the chair, he looked at Hayden. "And we're going to have to come back to that eventually, because even though I'm here watching the rear and Kelsie is keeping an eye out front, that may not be enough. If Mia's seen this woman twice, then it's pretty clear somebody knows y'all ran here. I'm going to recommend a safe house, even though you rejected the idea the first eight times I suggested it."

Would an unfamiliar place really be the best for Ruthie? "I don't know if—"

Elliott held up a hand to silence Hayden's protest. "That's a conversation for later. Right now, you've got some muck in your head that you need to clear out before we try to get tactical. Otherwise, you'll overwhelm and short-circuit. That's how bad decisions are made."

Hayden ran his finger along a rough spot in the plastic chair arm, ashamed that Elliott was right. He needed to release the valve on the thoughts and emotions he was desperately trying to cram into a pipe that had already burst. "It's Mia."

"I figured."

"Her husband and I were best friends our whole lives, and Mia was a part of that friendship almost as long." He wrapped his fingers around the chair arm. "How can I be feeling things for my best friend's wife? For my best friend now?"

"Well, first of all, we need to work on your terminology and maybe your slightly off-center sense of morality."

"What?" Hayden sputtered. "My off-center morality?"

"I said what I said." Elliott chuckled, then grew quiet. Long moments passed before he spoke again. "McGrath, as hard as this has been and still is, you and Mia both have to accept that Keith isn't coming back. While I'm sure Mia will always love him, he's no longer here. There is absolutely nothing wrong with having feelings for her."

The words hit so hard, Hayden flinched. He stared at the rarely used charcoal grill at the corner of the patio. It was the same kind his dad had used up until he'd passed away seven years ago from a sudden heart attack. Recognizing the childhood nostalgia that would link him to memories of his father, Mia had bought the grill as a housewarming gift when he'd moved in.

She was threaded through so much of his past and his present. Chances were high it would ruin him if he had to untangle her from his future.

Funny, but he couldn't see anything past today, had never let himself think about tomorrow. "After Keith died, I stopped caring about what came next. He didn't get another day. He had plans with Mia. They'd just adopted Ruthie. They had so many dreams, and every one of them was gunned down without warning." He continued to study the grill, draped in a canvas cover that kept it safe but attested to the little enjoyment he got out of it, since he never had the time to use it. "Just a few months later, Beth walked out. She took all of my dreams with her."

"Did she? Or did you lock them away from her?"

He ought to take offense at the insinuation that he'd destroyed his own relationship, but the words sank deep and heavy, dampening his anger.

Hayden pulled a piece of plastic from the chair. Had he pushed Beth away? He'd always assumed she'd been too weak to handle the grief they were walking through, had run at the first signs of struggle but... "I was spending a lot of time helping Mia with Ruthie. I was..." He clamped his back teeth together as memories shoved out of the closet where he'd locked them.

The arguments about setting a wedding date, picking a venue, finding a house...

In the wake of Keith's death, Hayden had stopped considering the future. The trauma of witnessing his best friend lying dead on the floor of a convenience store had shaken his life off its foundation. He'd fallen into a hopeless funk, unable to consider a future that might be violently ripped away. All of Beth's talk of weddings and houses had seemed trivial and foolish.

But they hadn't been trivial or foolish to Beth. The realization almost doubled him over. He pressed his hands against his stomach to keep it from making a run out of his body. Beth had wanted a future with him, had needed reassurance that he still wanted one with her, but he'd been so closed off in his grief, so focused on making sure his goddaughter and his friend were surviving, that he'd neglected the woman who loved him.

Then he'd blamed her when she'd chosen a life path that

wasn't marred by his inability to love her in the way she deserved.

Sick pain muddied his veins. He'd hurt her so badly. How had he never seen it?

He should apologize, but there was no way to make this right. Beth had married a teacher in Dare County two years earlier and lived on Hatteras Island now, where she worked for a real estate company in Avon. She was happy with a man who'd made her his world and cared about her feelings, as she deserved. He'd have to pray about reaching out to her, but she definitely needed some form of apology, because he'd stopped considering her when he'd nearly drowned in his grief.

"It might be time to start thinking about what your future looks like. You're still here and breathing. So is Mia. Neither of you can close the book and call your story done. You say you believe in God, and you're always talking about Him like He's a part of you. Maybe you need to think about why the guy upstairs still has you here." Elliott had always scoffed when anyone spoke of Jesus, but clearly, he'd been listening.

Elliott pulled his feet closer and stood, looking down at Hayden. "Brother, let me tell you something. I know you're struggling with taking on Keith's case for the relook, but I think you're the exact right person. Maybe your closure is going to come when you face his death head-on and truly grieve it. You walked Mia through it, but you never felt it for yourself. You internalized it and you hid from it. Watch the video, McGrath. It won't be easy, but it's necessary." With a cuff to the side of Hayden's head, Elliott walked away, disappearing around the side of the house.

Hayden rubbed the side of his head, then slumped in his chair. This was too much revelation for one night. He'd kissed Mia, and frankly, he'd enjoyed it up until guilt took a baseball bat to the back of his head. He also needed to deal with the fact that they might have been tracked to his house, and now he was being asked to confront the past as well.

It was overwhelming.

He rocketed to his feet, restless and needing to move. He had to do something.

Maybe Elliott was right. Maybe he needed to stop hiding from the hard things. The only way to do that was to do the most difficult thing he could imagine.

To turn on his computer and watch his best friend die.

Mia bent forward on the carpet and wrapped her arms around her legs. Pressing her head against her knees, she rocked on the floor beside the bed, fighting tremors that threatened to rip her apart. Tonight had been too much. Everything was just…too…much.

Emotions swamped her. Her fingers and toes went numb. Her heart stuttered. Her mind raced even faster than her pulse. Her teeth knocked together as though she was freezing, yet her skin was hot. She couldn't function another second.

The walls were closing in.

The woman at the Christmas lights. The whiplash of feeling safe and then facing danger.

Kissing her best friend.

Mia whimpered and leaped to her feet, wobbling as her balance struggled to catch up. Grabbing the corner of the nightstand, she held on until the room stopped spinning. As soon as her feet felt secure, she paced the room, her arms wrapped around her stomach.

She had enough to process without diving into that kiss and the way it had made her feel. For a moment, she'd forgotten everything except Hayden, and it had been…freeing.

It had also been completely out of control.

Out of control was bad.

She needed to get out. To run. To breathe fresh air.

But Hayden's alarm system was even better than hers, and she'd heard him engage it a few moments earlier, when the keypad in his room down the hall beeped confirmation that he'd armed the system. Even opening a window could set off an alarm that would awaken Ruthie or bring Hayden's armed teammates on the run.

God, help me. It felt as though her skeleton was going to leap from her skin. She fought for breath, crying out silent prayers.

Please make it stop.

When she finally figured out her central fear, the cries of her heart poured forth. *Make it stop. All of it.* The panic attacks. The fear. The physical assaults on her family. *God, make it stop. You have the ability. You're God. All-powerful. All-knowing. Snap Your finger. Say the word. Just...make it stop.*

Once the words were out, the tears followed, and the tension in her body released. She dropped to the edge of the bed and fell onto her back, staring at the ceiling as tears ran into her ears. Anger replaced the fear, and the desire to pray evaporated. How mean was a God who could take away her pain but chose not to?

I don't want to talk to You. She felt like Ruthie in full hissy fit mode. If she crossed her arms and stomped her foot, the transformation would be complete.

She no longer cared if she looked immature or silly. This wasn't the first time she'd railed at God. It wouldn't be the last. Everything was so unfair. Hadn't they been through enough?

Rocketing to her feet, Mia headed for the door on autopilot. She needed water. Food. Anything to distract her from her thoughts. There would be no sleep anytime soon, even given how spent she was after a full-blown panic attack.

At the door, Mia stopped with her hand on the cool metal knob. If she went downstairs, she ran a 100 percent risk of seeing Hayden.

Could she face him?

Claustrophobia beat humiliation. She had to get out of this room, maybe talk Hayden into letting her sit outside for a few minutes. His friends would protect her. She just needed air.

She crept down the stairs, trying not to disturb him if he'd fallen asleep on the couch. Even if he hadn't, maybe she could sneak into the kitchen without him noticing. Given the house's open floor plan, that was likely impossible, but a girl could dream.

Could she handle looking him in the eye so soon after…? When she couldn't even articulate the feelings spinning inside of her? When she had no idea if that kiss had been a re-action to trauma or if it had been very, very real?

Because it sure had felt real.

When she reached the bottom of the stairs, the space was empty. Mia stepped into the living room, her brow furrowed. Every light in the downstairs was on, even the decorative lamp on the built-in bookshelf. It was as though Hayden had a compulsive need to dispel every shadow in the house.

The kitchen lights were ablaze as well. Her cheek twitched as tears stung her eyes. Sometimes she forgot that Hayden suffered, too. That he'd been present on the night Keith died. That he'd lost his best friend just as surely as she'd lost hers.

His amped-up alarm system was a silent testament to the inner turmoil he felt but rarely spoke. Maybe he normally kept all of the lights on, vainly trying to keep the darkness of night from creeping into his home.

But where was he? She'd heard him arm the alarm system,

and he'd never come upstairs. His bedroom door was open, and the room had been dark when she passed.

She turned a slow circle and paused when she faced the front door. On the right side of the entry was an open dining room that he used as a man cave, where various military awards and photos were displayed. On the left side of the entry was a small office with French doors and built-in bookshelves. He must be in there.

The kitchen was behind her. Hayden was in front of her. She could easily slip in, get something to drink, hide until she regained her equilibrium, then sneak back upstairs. That would be taking care of herself, and no one would fault her.

Or, she could face her best friend despite the awkwardness and ask how he was doing. If she was spinning out of control, then he was likely feeling the vertigo of the past few days as well. That would be taking care of someone else.

For once, she needed to do the selfless thing.

Steeling herself against the sight of him, she pressed her fingers to her lips in a vain attempt to erase the sensation of his kiss, then walked toward the door.

When she peeked into the office, Hayden was sitting at his oversize wooden desk facing the door, his head buried in his hands and his laptop open before him. It was a posture of hopelessness and defeat.

She'd done this to him. She'd dragged him into her world of fear and had forced him and his coworkers to protect her from a stalker... No, two stalkers.

Her heart ached. Maybe she should reach out to the police, although that would do no good. The crimes in Wincombe were under Tyrrell County's jurisdiction, and they were already being investigated. There'd been no actual crime tonight, although the woman was certainly suspicious and possibly dangerous. Still, there had to be some way to free

Hayden from having to worry about her. Maybe she could take Ruthie to her grandmother's house in the mountains. Would they be safe there?

As she backed away from the door, the hardwood floor creaked.

Hayden's head jerked up, his hands rushing to close his laptop. "Mia." He exhaled roughly. "I didn't know what that noise was."

"Sorry. I didn't mean to scare you. I was feeling trapped upstairs and came down for some water. I shouldn't have bothered you." It was the last thing she'd wanted.

He slid the laptop aside, staring at it for a long time before he looked at her. "You can come in." He flicked his index finger toward one of the comfy leather chairs in front of the desk. "I'd rather not work tonight anyway."

Mia crept into the room and sat on the edge of the chair. *Work.* That meant… "Keith's case?" Until now, she'd forgotten he was heading up the reinvestigation.

His expression clouded, but he nodded.

She'd been right. He was suffering as much as she was, though his pain took on a different cast than hers. He wore the same veil of grief that he'd worn at her house the night before. Both times, he'd had his laptop in front of him.

Her eyes narrowed, and her stomach clenched. There was something about his laptop, something that disturbed him. "What files are you working on?"

He stared at her, his expression guarded. Deep lines furrowed his forehead. "I don't know that you want to have this conversation."

"Maybe it's not about me. Maybe you need to."

"I can't do that to you."

"You know, sometimes I get tired of being the weak one." A surge of strength charged through her. "You try to carry all of my hurts and fears as well as your own and…maybe it would be good for both of us if *I* took on some of what *you're* carrying for once. Maybe it would stop you from feeling so weighed down, and maybe it would stop me from feeling like such a burden."

"You are not a burden." His answer was quick and firm. "I have never once thought that. Being your friend is a privilege, Mia."

"Same to you. So let me share the privilege." She leaned forward, finding strength in letting go of herself to focus on him. "What's on the laptop?"

He shook his head.

"Hayden…" It was the same voice she used on Ruthie when her daughter was trying to tell a fib.

His shoulders slumped. "Elliott got the…security footage." It was clear the confession cost him.

That was it? They'd both viewed surveillance tapes dozens if not hundreds of times. Had watched so many hours of—

No.

The meaning of his words ran molten lead over her head, down her shoulders and to her feet.

Security footage.

Her gaze landed on the laptop and refused to break away.

On that machine were images of her husband's last breath. Of their helpless baby girl in the carrier beside him. Of his blood. Of her first moments of grief.

Her breath caught. The moment her life had changed forever, had shattered into blood-spattered shards, was in the room with her, stealing the air.

She jerked her head, tearing her gaze from the laptop and landing on Hayden, who was watching her. The exact same emotions that ripped through her were plain on his face. They'd experienced that night together. Had suffered the tearing pain of loss together. Should they view that moment together as well?

Could she? If she fell apart now, she might never recover, and she'd be a burden to her best friend for the rest of their lives.

Hayden needed her, and she needed to be the strong one. If sitting beside him while he watched that footage would help him, she would. She'd do anything for him, just like she'd do anything for her daughter.

Just like she'd have done anything for Keith.

The realization settled like a warm blanket, something she'd always known but had never acknowledged.

Something that made their earlier kiss even more poignant.

Before she could make the offer, Hayden reached for the laptop, then pulled his hand away as though it was too hot to touch. "I've tried to watch it twice now, but I don't think I can."

If he was going to stay on this case, he'd have to face this. How could he—

Something thudded above her head in Ruthie's room.

Mia and Hayden leaped to their feet, and Mia whirled toward the door as Ruthie screamed.

ELEVEN

"Mommy!" Ruthie's terrified cries echoed along the hallway.

Hayden gripped the Glock he'd grabbed from his locked desk drawer and held it low, his finger down the side of the barrel. It was likely Ruthie had simply had a nightmare, though he was pretty sure she'd never had one before.

Given all that had happened, he wasn't taking any chances.

The door chime beeped, then the alarm blared, adding to the cacophony of sound both outside and inside of Hayden. Either Elliott and Kelsie had rushed in to help or someone was trying to escape.

No, it couldn't be an escape. If there was an intruder, the person would have had to pass them on the stairs.

But how did they get inside in the first place?

There was a series of beeps as someone keyed in the alarm's code, and the siren fell silent. It was definitely Elliott or Kelsie who had entered.

"Mommy!" Ruthie screamed again. Her bedroom door flew open, and a tiny rocket dressed in *PAW Patrol* pajamas streaked past him. His goddaughter threw herself into her mother's arms, sobbing.

At least she was safe.

Mia gathered the shaking little girl to her chest and whis-

pered soothing sounds that had no actual words in them,
just comfort.

Now wasn't the time to huddle in the hallway in the open.
While it might have been a nightmare, there could also be
an active threat.

Hayden hissed at Mia, "Get her downstairs and secured
in the laundry room." The small space had no windows, and
it was the best he could do for a safe room in a pinch.

Mia headed for the stairs with Ruthie, where Elliott and
Kelsie pounded up, weapons drawn. By some unspoken conversation, Kelsie ushered Mia and Ruthie downstairs while
Elliott approached Hayden and took up a position against
the wall to his left. "Status?"

"Not sure, but I really hope we're overreacting to a little
girl's nightmare." While Ruthie didn't typically have bad
dreams, she'd been through a lot in the past thirty-six hours
or so. Her emotions had to be overwhelmed.

In his pocket, his cell phone buzzed, likely the alarm company checking on the alert. He ignored it. If he didn't answer,
they'd send the police, and that was just fine.

Hayden nodded toward Ruthie's door. "Let's go find out
what we're dealing with." He crept along the wall as Elliott
covered him, then entered the room, weapon raised.

Ruthie's night-light swept dots of light across the ceiling, mimicking stars. The shifting light cast moving shadows on the walls and floor, making it tough to discern what
was real and what was a figment of his racing imagination.
As his eyes adjusted, the shadows revealed no visible threat,
although the room was unusually chilly.

He cleared the area and moved on to the bathroom as Elliott followed, checking the closet and under the bed.

No one was in the room.

But why was it so cold?

Hayden stalked to the window and jerked back the curtain.

The window was open. The screen had been removed and was leaning against the wall, hidden behind the floor-length curtains. The emergency fire ladder he'd anchored beneath the window was unrolled down the side of the house and was still swinging from the weight of a hasty exit.

"How?" He resisted the urge to shut the window, not wanting to mar any prints that may have been left behind. He closed the curtains and motioned for Elliott to flick on the switch, flooding the room with light. "How did somebody get past me? Past you? You and Kelsie have been outside the whole time, watching the front and back. There aren't any side doors. The only way…"

Hayden pulled his phone out. He texted Kelsie to shelter in place and to notify the police that this was not a false alarm. Pocketing the phone, he turned to Elliott, who watched from the bathroom door. "We have to clear the house."

Elliott offered a grim nod, then moved out, taking the two bedrooms on the left while Hayden took his bedroom on the right.

The only way someone had managed to get into Ruthie's room without being seen was if they had gained entry to the house while everyone was at the light show.

Hayden swallowed self-recrimination, forcing himself to focus on the job as he checked every possible hiding place. He followed Elliott downstairs, where they searched every nook, cranny and shadowy space.

Elliott met him in the living room, holstering his sidearm as he approached. "All clear."

Hayden lowered his Glock, then texted Kelsie to keep Mia and Ruthie in the laundry room a bit longer, not wanting the little girl further upset by the arrival of police officers.

From the laundry room, the sound of Ruthie's muffled sobs drifted into the den.

Hayden's heart tugged in that direction. He wanted to pick Ruthie up, cuddle her close and comfort her, but she was safe with her mother. Mia was the only comfort Ruthie needed, even though Hayden's heart ached to reach out.

He should secure his weapon before the police arrived, since he hadn't grabbed the holster. With Elliott and Kelsie both armed, he didn't need it for protection at the moment. Stalking into his office, he locked the gun in the reinforced top desk drawer and pocketed the key.

When he was done, he turned to find Elliott in the doorway, concern pouring off him. "What happened?"

"I don't know." Hayden sank into his chair, an adrenaline crash stealing the strength from his legs. "Somebody got into the house while we were gone."

"That's next to impossible." Elliott's dark eyebrows drew together, narrowing his brown eyes. "Your system rivals any bank's. Frankly, it's overkill, but I get it, after what you've been through."

Elliott was right. His alarm was a powerful system for a house that had little of value in it, but Keith's death had been a grim wake-up call that no place was truly safe. Frankly, after the past thirty-six hours, he felt like putting metal bars on the windows and never leaving again.

This must be how Mia felt every day. Like everything was a catalyst for fear. Like the world was out to destroy her.

Sympathy swelled in his chest, but he forced himself to focus. This mystery demanded answers. "My code's a meaningless series of numbers chosen by a random number generator. I know better than to use a birthday or something easy to guess."

Blue and white flashing lights reflected against the curtains, indicating the police had arrived with their sirens silent.

Hayden didn't move. He was empty. Exhausted.

Elliott backed into the entry, prepared to open the door when the knock came. "Any other way to shut the system off? Remote? Phone app?"

"I have an app on my phone, but…" Hayden stood as a horrible thought rushed in. "Maybe someone managed to hack my account. They could have downloaded the app and used it to disarm the system."

That would have required a sophisticated hack, but it wasn't impossible.

Had his first line of defense been compromised?

Mia was right.

Nowhere was safe.

Ruthie's arm rose and fell with her breathing, which had finally evened out after an hour of intermittent sobs.

Mia gently relaxed against the back of the couch, one hand resting on her daughter's arm where it was draped across her little stomach. Her other hand lay on top of Ruthie's head in her lap.

It was just after midnight. Dawn would come sooner than she wanted. As much as she was terrified of the dark, she hated to imagine what the coming day would bring.

She'd overheard Hayden talking to Elliott about moving to a safe house.

Mia bit down on what would surely be a harsh laugh. *Safe* was an illusion. That truth had hammered itself into her soul the moment Keith had breathed his last. Everything that had happened since she'd spotted the mysterious woman at lunch on Saturday only confirmed that danger lurked everywhere and could reach her whenever it chose.

The back door in the kitchen opened, then the alarm beeped as someone punched in the lock code. Hayden stepped into the arched opening quietly, obviously checking to see if she was asleep.

She offered him a weak smile, then tipped her chin toward Ruthie, whose quiet breathing was occasionally interrupted by an almost imperceptible snore that indicated she was down for the count. When she slept that hard, not even a hurricane could awaken her.

Boy, did Mia envy that kind of rest.

Hayden walked in, snagged a blanket off the back of his recliner and draped the covering gently over Ruthie before he sat down on the coffee table facing Mia. "You okay?"

"Did you really ask me a question you already know the answer to?"

"I did." He wrinkled his nose. "And yeah, I guess the answer is pretty obvious. You're no more okay than I am."

"What happens now?" The Elizabeth City police officers who had responded had taken statements from them all. One plain-clothed female officer had even sat with Ruthie over mugs of hot chocolate to talk in a gentle way about what had frightened her.

Ruthie's eyes had welled with tears as she'd shrunk against her mother. "A ghost. A shadow ghost." It had taken a bit more coaxing to get a firm description out of the little girl, whose senses had been hindered by her moving night-light and her fear. After a few more questions, Ruthie was able to articulate that the person in her room had been wearing dark pants and a dark hoodie. She had been unable to tell if it was a male or a female. The person had said nothing, had simply appeared in her doorway and approached her bed.

If Ruthie had been asleep instead of up playing with her night-light...

Mia swallowed a whimper. Had her daughter been asleep, then her would-be kidnapper likely would have had her gagged and out the window before Ruthie could have alerted them.

How close had she come to losing her daughter tonight— twice?

"Hey." Hayden's voice drew her out of her fear-soaked imagination. He leaned forward and rested his hand on her knee. "We're going to handle this."

Digging her teeth into her tongue, Mia forced herself to remain silent. So far, nobody had a *handle* on anything.

That wasn't Hayden's fault. Someone savvy was coming after them, but she couldn't wrap her mind around the clues to discern who it might be. "I should be able to figure this out." She'd been a soldier and a deputy, yet any time she tried to think tactically, her mind turned to mush. It was further proof that she would never again be who she once was. She'd always be a hindrance and never a help.

It was also proof that the kiss with Hayden never should have happened.

"Hold up. This is not yours to *figure out*." Hayden pulled his hand away and rested his palms on his knees. "Your sole job in this moment is to be Ruthie's mother. Not a law enforcement officer. Not a soldier. You're the only one in the world who can do that."

"Not according to whoever tackled me in Watchman's Alley." The words slipped past the filter in her brain. Maybe she was failing as a mom. After all, she'd let her daughter be approached by a strange woman, had nearly let someone steal Ruthie right from under her nose, had—

"Whatever you're thinking, stop." Although he didn't touch her, Hayden leaned closer. "You're a great mom, and despite what you think, you're also a great friend. I wouldn't have made it through the past few years without you. You might think you need me, but I…" He looked away. His eyebrows drew together into a deep V, and he shook his head. "I'm sorry about earlier, between me and you. I'm not sure what happened, but it won't happen again." He abruptly stood, looking down at her. "You asked a couple of minutes ago what happens now."

The whiplash from the conversational turn threw Mia off balance, as though his words had affected her equilibrium. How had they moved from her being a mother to their friendship to the kiss to…? Was he talking about what happened next in their relationship or what happened next with the battle around them?

Clearly, his apology for the kiss meant this was about the danger. As much as his regret over their kiss twisted her stomach into knots, she knew he was right. Ruthie's safety had to be their focus.

Digging deep, she sought the strength to move forward.

All she found was emptiness. She'd gone completely numb.

That was worse than fear, but at least it allowed her to think. "We're leaving, aren't we?"

"Elliott's firming up arrangements for a safe house, and we're figuring out how to move the two of you without being tracked." He walked to the kitchen entry and stared in the direction of the back door. "They knew you were here. Worse, I talked to my alarm company. At shortly after five this evening, someone deactivated my alarm from a cell phone app and then reactivated it approximately one minute later. They hacked my house."

Mia eased away from Ruthie and stood, the law enforcement part of her brain engaged. She walked into the kitchen to avoid waking her daughter. "That means they were in the house for over an hour before we got home."

"Which means the woman you saw tonight wasn't the person in the house. We definitely have two people in play here, if—" He didn't look at her.

But she heard him loud and clear. "If I really did see the same woman from the café." His skepticism was understandable. If she was standing in his shoes, she'd feel it as well. Still... "I have no doubt she was the same person. The question is who she is and how she knew where to find us."

"And was she the person in the alley?"

"And who was in the house?" Mia slid onto the stool by the peninsula and buried her head in her hands. So much to consider. "I really don't want to move Ruthie to a safe house. It's technically Christmas Eve. All of her presents are here, and she's more concerned about Santa than anything else. This constant shuffling seems cruel."

When Hayden didn't speak, she lifted her head.

He was staring at the back door as though waiting for someone to come through it. When he realized she was watching, he shifted his gaze to her without moving. "I get it, but..." He exhaled heavily, dragging his hands down cheeks thick with a couple of days' worth of stubble. "There's more."

Mia closed her eyes. She was pretty sure she couldn't bear the load of *more*. "Is it about Paige?"

"Not exactly." Hayden walked to the other side of the peninsula and faced her. "Based on what you told me about your interactions with Paige's family yesterday, Javi and some of the other deputies have been looking into the people who were at the Crosby home who might have the most interest in you and Ruthie."

"Paige's father and her boyfriend." Cade had never been for the adoption, and Blake had acted so strangely, even though he'd signed away his parental rights. Maybe he'd changed his mind. "Who do they suspect?"

"Cade is still at the house. He's been there since he arrived after news of Paige's disappearance, and he was definitely in Wilmington when she vanished."

Mia felt a slight sense of relief. At least she could let go of any suspicion that Cade had killed his own daughter. "And Blake?"

"He hasn't been seen since he walked out of the house. His cell is off, and his vehicle didn't have GPS, so there's no way to track it."

Mia slumped in the seat. Blake had always been friendly. Had he been hiding dark motives? She couldn't fathom someone who cared so much about Paige harming her. But... "Blake knows you and I are friends. He knows you were at the house with me. It wouldn't take much for him to figure out where we ran." It would also explain the comments from her attacker about her as a mother, particularly if Blake wanted to raise Ruthie.

"But it doesn't explain the mystery woman."

No, it didn't. "Maybe I really am so paranoid that I..." *No.* Surely her fear hadn't started causing her to hallucinate. As a law enforcement officer, she'd been trained to notice details about people. This woman had a scar on her temple and blond hair. Although it was full and clean now, her hair had once been—

Mia sat straight up. The scar. The hair. When the woman had walked into her memory just now, it wasn't with the lovely blond hair she had in the present. It was straighter. Stringier. And in Mia's memory, she was thin to the point of emaciated.

Mia gasped. "Hayden. I know who she is. I don't know how she found us, but I know who she is."

Tears pricked her eyes, and she pressed a finger to her lips, remembering that day. It had been her first week on the job as a deputy, and the Department of Social Services had requested law enforcement presence as they removed a three-year-old from the home of an addict who'd repeatedly been cited for neglect and abuse. The woman had grown violent, screaming and hitting anyone who came near as they carried her daughter, who seemed to have no emotional attachment to her mother, away from the home.

The woman had been handcuffed and arrested for her behavior, and as Deputy Anna Titus shut the car door on the woman, she'd turned to Mia, who'd been horrified by the scene, heartbroken for both mother and daughter. Anna had said, "That kid deserves better than her."

Mia related the story to Hayden. "She must have remembered me and blamed me for taking her daughter. Maybe she thought I said those awful things, then when she saw me at the café…"

Hayden reached for his back pocket, producing his cell. "Do you remember her name?"

Mia shook her head. "I only heard it once or twice. You'd think it would have been burned into my brain. It's in the reports. It was like my fourth or fifth day on the job." She tossed out a couple of dates. "Sheriff Davidson should be able to pull up the details."

Hayden dialed the phone and walked toward the back door, speaking in low tones, as Mia stared at her fingers, twined together on the counter. Was it going to be that simple? Was this all about revenge?

TWELVE

"Her name is Jasmine Jarrett. I've sent her photo to each of you." Hayden pocketed the backup phone Elliott had brought him and looked around at his team, who had packed into his office. When Elliott had called Gavin and Rebecca, they'd returned. Along with Kelsie and Elliott, that made four extra sets of eyes and ears. Their unconditional willingness to protect him and the people he loved both warmed him and unsettled him.

They were rolling out in a few minutes for the safe house that Elliott had arranged. A buddy of his had a condo on the waterfront in Manteo, and, as long as they could get Mia and Ruthie there without detection, it should be difficult for anyone to locate them. He had the burner phone from Elliott, and Mia had already left her phone at her house. They'd moved Ruthie's car seat into a pickup they'd borrowed from Gavin. There should be no way to track them.

He'd made a tactical error in bringing them to his house when so many people knew he was linked to Mia. It was a mistake that could have cost them their lives.

As he glanced around the small circle, it was clear his friends and coworkers were as exhausted as he was. He honestly couldn't remember the last time he'd slept. Gavin and Rebecca had likely only gotten a couple of hours before Elliott had called them to see if they wanted to help, and there was no telling how long Kelsie and Elliott had been awake, given that they were already on night shift when everything fell apart.

Gratitude nearly knocked him off his worn-out feet. They'd sacrificed so much for him, and he was basically still the rookie on the team. He waited for everyone to check the photos he'd sent to their phones before he spoke. He had to clear his throat to get the words out. "I, um… Thanks. I know you could be anywhere else right now. I want you to know I appreciate you being here."

Rebecca bumped her shoulder against his. "My parents are in Hawaii on vacation. There is nowhere else I'd rather be right now than making sure that adorable little girl gets where we're going safely." They'd been careful not to mention their destination aloud, fearful of somehow being overheard.

"Ditto." Kelsie slid her cell into her hip pocket. Her brown ponytail fell over her shoulder with the movement. "I mean, my parents aren't in Hawaii, but ditto on the rest of that."

Elliott and Gavin grunted their responses.

"Still. It can't be—"

"Knock it off, McGrath." Elliott heaved an exaggerated sigh. "We get it. Now let's get this caravan rolling. Sooner we have everyone settled, sooner we can rest." He looked around at the assembled group. "Kelsie and I will take my truck and leave three minutes ahead of you, keeping an eye out for anything suspicious on the route and making sure it's clear. If you drive exactly three miles over the speed limit, we should maintain an even distance." He tipped his head toward Rebecca. "Rebecca, you and Gavin follow Hayden. Keep him in sight at all times, and watch behind you as well. We don't know how many bad actors are in play or how Jasmine Jarrett found Mia and Ruthie to begin with. We have no clue what might come at us next. All we know is that Jasmine's parole officer hasn't seen her in several weeks, and it's entirely possible she wants to take Ruthie as a way to punish Mia."

"Or to get what she feels she's owed. A kid." The thought turned Hayden's stomach. Whatever Jasmine Jarrett wanted with Ruthie, it wasn't good. He just hoped the BOLO they'd put out on her for parole violations would lead to a quick apprehension. "But why wait this long?" *And how did she know Mia had a daughter?*

"Too many questions, not enough moving toward the vehicles. Let's go." Elliott was in mission mode and ready to roll. Investigations could come later, when everyone was safe.

As the team headed out the front door, Hayden went into the den where Mia sat on the couch at Ruthie's feet, watching her daughter sleep. She'd packed their things, including Ruthie's Christmas presents, and Hayden had loaded them into the borrowed truck a few minutes earlier. All that remained now was to get Ruthie to the car and to get on the road.

Without a word, Mia gathered her sleeping daughter in her arms and preceded Hayden out the door. When she buckled Ruthie into her car seat and tucked Penelope into her arms, the little girl barely stirred.

Watching through the driver's side rear window, Hayden allowed himself a short moment for the scene to work its way into his heart. He couldn't deny that he loved Ruthie like she was his own daughter.

Could he deny that he loved Mia as though she was his own as well?

Shaking off the thought, he climbed into the front seat as Mia slid in and buckled up. No matter what Elliott said, the thought of being in love with Mia still felt odd.

Odd, but right.

It was also a distraction he needed to set aside if he wanted a future to contemplate.

As Hayden watched Elliott back out and drive up the street, the truck was silent except for the vents blowing warm air. He waited three minutes before following Elliott. He knew the route to Manteo well, and he could practically drive it in his sleep.

Given that he hadn't shut his eyes in what felt like two years, he might have to. He was weary to the bone, yet his brain was amped and running through everything that could go wrong, all of the ways he could lose the people he cared about most.

"Are you going to watch the surveillance footage?" Mia's voice broke the silence so suddenly yet so softly, he almost wondered if he'd dropped off and was dreaming.

Long seconds passed before he comprehended her question. She was picking up their earlier conversation from the point when Ruthie's screams had interrupted them.

"Is this something we want to talk about now?" He'd prefer to save emotional discussions for another time.

"We have a long, dark drive ahead of us. Seems like as good a time as any. It's something you need to work through, and… I want to work through it with you. I don't want you to do this alone."

Her concern nearly unraveled him. He focused on the turn out of his neighborhood, considering what she was asking. The darkness and their inability to look each other in the eye as he drove lent a sense of anonymity to the moment, a detachment he wouldn't find anywhere else.

She might be right. This might be the best time to work through his emotions.

Did he want to watch the footage? The details were already seared into his brain and often plowed through his sleep, awakening him in a cold sweat.

Keith's motionless body, eyes wide and unseeing.

The metallic scent of blood.

Mia's cries as she held infant Ruthie and clung to Hayden.

The hopeless feeling of being too late, compounded by the sting of allowing Keith's killer to escape.

Did he really need the image of the bullet's impact imprinted on his brain?

"If I watch the video, it will add one more scene to my nightmares." He pulled his eyes from the dark road to look at her. "If I wasn't a factor, would you watch it?"

Mia's face was lit only by the dim lights of the instrument panel. Deep lines etched her forehead. Pain and fear had carved those lines.

He'd do anything to take them away.

Finally, she shook her head. "No." She offered no explanation.

She didn't need to. One word said enough.

At least for her. For him, the words bubbled up, needing release. "Elliott thinks I won't heal unless I watch it. And honestly, I'm the only one on the team who was there that night, who can give insight into—"

"Maybe Elliott's wrong."

The quiet words seemed to pick up speed, slamming into him at terminal velocity. His grip on the wheel tightened. Elliott...*wrong*? The man was a logical machine. One of the most well-thought-out people Hayden had ever known. His insights usually hit the mark, and his people trusted him for guidance. How could he be *wrong*?

"No offense to Elliott." Mia looked over her shoulder at her sleeping daughter, then turned her gaze to Hayden. "He's a great person, and he seems to care about all of you.

I mean, how many people would do what he's doing for me and Ruthie, and he doesn't know us at all. But being a good person and caring about the people around you doesn't mean you're right a hundred percent of the time."

Maybe? But if that was the case... "Then who do I trust?"

"God first. And then, in a situation like this, yourself." She pulled one of his hands from the wheel and laced her fingers with his, resting on the console between them. "Hay, at some point, you have to stop second-guessing yourself. Maybe Elliott's path to healing is to know every detail, to file away every image so he has no questions. But you aren't Elliott. It would..." Her fingers tightened. "It would destroy me to watch what that camera picked up. My memories are bad enough. I think your memories are bad enough for you, too."

Hayden looked up in time to see the lights of a passing vehicle glisten in tears that stood in her eyes. The urge to pull off to the side of the road and hold her nearly overwhelmed him. He had to wrestle himself into submission to stick to the plan.

Mia sniffed, then swiped her eyes. "You're not solely responsible for bringing Keith's killer to justice, especially not if it's going to cause you harm. I don't think I could handle it if you watched the footage and it changed you."

His breath caught. Her words flowed on raw emotion.

"Hayden, you're human. One of the greatest guilts I carry is that you spend all of your time taking care of me and of Ruthie. I'm not sure you've ever really stopped to confront your own grief. You lost your best friend. You were a victim that night just as much as I was. You don't have to be the strongest man alive. You just have to be you, and you have to feel this in your own way or you're never going to heal."

The truth watered his dry spirit. The raging forest fire

he'd felt for so many years was doused. His mind and emotions fell silent.

He was allowed to let go. Allowed to be angry and sad and scared.

He didn't need to power through. He didn't need to be the hero who saved the day. He was allowed to protect his own heart as well as Mia's.

The sense of peace that replaced the inferno within him was startling after so many years of smoke and flame. "I don't have to do this by myself." His left hand gripped the steering wheel tighter, and he tugged his right from Mia's grasp. That was something he hadn't meant to say aloud. While he didn't need to carry everything, neither did she. How dare he add to her burden?

"You were never supposed to do this alone. I mean, you have God. You have…" She looked away. Trees passed in the darkness as they left civilization behind. "You have me."

The tough cop, tough soldier, that lived deep inside of Mia cringed. *You have me.* She sounded like a sound bite from the trailer for a Christmas romance movie. They were driving through the darkness, fleeing for their lives, and she was talking like they were in a horse-drawn carriage on a snow-covered lane.

Thankfully the truck was dark so Hayden couldn't see the bright red glow that burned her cheeks.

She dug her teeth into her tongue to keep her from saying another word. Maybe he hadn't heard.

The problem was her brain. It had been running five hundred miles per hour for too long and was dangerously close to short-circuiting. The assault at Watchman's Alley, the arson attempt at her home, the breach at Hayden's… Everything increased the power until her system was running in the red.

And Hayden had kissed her. That event slammed on the brakes, though the engine still fired. With Ruthie's screams following so quickly after that brain-shattering moment, she had lost control of her feelings and her thoughts and the ability to censor herself.

She was out of control.

She had two choices. Either she focused on Hayden and his issues, or she popped the clutch and spun into a panic attack that might actually engulf her. She could feel it building, pounding, threatening.

The only way to stop it was to distract it with someone else's problems.

But she'd gone too far and inserted herself into the narrative. Now Hayden would know she'd been affected not just by his kiss but by every action he'd taken on her behalf in the past four years. She could see it all now, stretched out like a string of Christmas lights. Each act of careful concern, of quiet listening, of fierce protectiveness, added a bulb in the strand that led from his heart to hers. The lights had been there all along, but that kiss had finally provided the electricity, giving power to a glorious riot of colors.

How could she be thinking this way when her daughter was in danger? Shouldn't her focus be on getting them to safety?

Her head whipped toward Hayden, who gripped the steering wheel with both hands and seemed to be wrestling with the effect of her words. No, she didn't have to focus on safety, because Hayden was doing that for her. Just like always. He was there when she needed him, every single time.

"I'm not sure what to say right now." Hayden kept his eyes on the road. "It's a lot. There's...a lot going on. Paige is dead, and you're being hunted... Now Blake is missing, and... And then there's you."

She wished he hadn't listed everything that was happening. It brought to the forefront that there was an evil outside of this truck that was launching terror and harm at her family. The danger drew her focus away from him and back to the reason for this flight through the darkness. It reminded her that there were legitimate reasons for her to be afraid.

This fight wasn't against shadows in her head. This was real.

Mia shoved her hands under her thighs and dug her fingers into her jeans. She had to clamp down and hold on or she might fly apart. She had to focus on something other than the danger, and she had to do it quickly. "We should talk about what happened."

He stiffened, and the tension radiating from him was palpable. "I can't right now. I have to get you to the safe house. Everything else is a distraction."

Her eyes drifted closed at the pain his words knifed through her. She was a distraction.

No matter that she was feeling things she couldn't explain for him, he viewed her as a hindrance. "I understand." She had no doubt he could hear every crack that splintered through her heart.

"Wait. No." Hayden's words rushed forth. "That came out wrong. We do need to talk. It's just that now isn't the time. I'm exhausted, Mia. And, frankly, I'm scared of a lot of things. From what's happening around you to what's happening… Well, to what's happening between us. My brain can only handle one thing at a time. That's all I'm saying. When we get settled where we're headed, we can—"

A soft hum cut off the rest of the sentence, and Mia straightened, her emotions going numb as Hayden's phone lit up in the cup holder between them. They had planned to be radio silent unless there was an emergency, in case who-

ever was stalking Mia had gained access to their communications. If a member of Hayden's team was calling, then
something terrible had happened.

Hayden picked up his phone and passed it to her. "Put it
on speaker. The volume is low enough to keep from waking Ruthie."

A slight warmth broke through her fear. He always thought
of Ruthie, of her, before anything else. As she swiped her
thumb along the screen beneath Elliott's name and punched
the speaker button, that warmth chilled. Her gut said she was
about to hear something that would change her life…again.

She held the phone close to Hayden, who leaned toward
it. "You're on speaker."

"Good. I want Mia to hear this. I just got a call from a
buddy on the Elizabeth City PD. They picked up Jasmine
Jarrett wandering down Halstead near 17. Apparently, she's
on a stratospheric high, babbling about a lot of stuff no one
can decipher. They're taking her to the ER in Elizabeth City."

The phone nearly fell from Mia's hand as relief ran
through her, but she lifted it quickly as Hayden spoke. "Can
we get someone there to talk to her?"

"You know we can't." Elliott's voice was clipped. "We're
not law enforcement, and we're not investigating this. We're
private citizens taking care of our own."

"Wishful thinking." Hayden tapped his thumbs on the
steering wheel. "I say we stay the course, continue on to
the safe house."

"Agreed. I'll let you know if anything else comes across."
The screen went dark as Elliott disconnected.

Mia lowered the phone into the cup holder and leaned
closer to Hayden after checking to be certain Ruthie still
slept. "'Stay the course'?" She hissed the words, trying not
to yell. "Jasmine Jarrett is in custody." Surely this was over.

They could turn around, get some rest at Hayden's and be home in time for Christmas Eve dinner with her grandmother, who was driving in from Flat Rock.

"Mia, stop thinking with your emotions," Hayden snapped, then winced when she flinched. He lowered his voice. "Jasmine Jarrett isn't our only concern. We don't know if the person in Watchman's Alley was a man or a woman. I fought a *man* at your house. The only thing we have on Jasmine Jarrett is that you saw her in a café and Ruthie was talking to her at a light show. Neither of those things is illegal."

Resting her elbow on the console, Mia pinched the bridge of her nose. She knew. Oh, did she know. But she wanted so badly to pretend. She wanted to go home, pull the blinds, sleep in her own bed… She wanted to stop feeling hunted and vulnerable.

But Jasmine's arrest wouldn't make those feelings go away. Putting an end to this threat wouldn't change anything. She'd been locked in fear and anxiety for four years. They were magnified now that the threat was real, but they'd likely still haunt her even after she was supposedly safe again.

"I understand what you're feeling." Hayden's voice was barely a whisper. "I want everything you're thinking about right now, too. I want to be home and safe and to have this all over."

He hadn't even had to ask. He just knew. "I'm scared." Not panicked. Genuinely scared.

"Me, too."

His quiet admission should have magnified the terror, but it had the opposite effect. The fact that he was frightened validated her emotions and made her feel…normal. She'd begged for *normal* for four years. Who'd have thought she'd find it in the midst of very real fear?

"Your lives are in my hands, and—" The phone buzzed in the cup holder.

Mia grabbed it and answered, turning on the speaker so Hayden could hear Rebecca.

Rebecca was midsentence when the call connected. "—got trouble. Someone is—" There was a screech and a shout, then silence.

THIRTEEN

"Call Elliott." Hayden rattled off the passcode to unlock the phone so that Mia could make the call. His heart rate picked up speed along with the truck as he pressed the accelerator to the floor. Behind him, Rebecca's car had fishtailed wildly before it disappeared.

Another set of headlights raced past the crash site, gaining fast.

Someone had run their tail off the road.

He had to catch up to Elliott and Kelsie before whoever had taken out Gavin and Rebecca could catch them. *Lord, let them be okay.* If a member of his team was hurt or worse because they were doing him a favor, he wasn't sure he could live with the guilt that would pile onto the load he already struggled to carry.

He glanced in the rearview as Mia dealt with the phone.

The headlights raced closer.

While he knew the road well, he didn't dare push the accelerator all the way to the floor. He couldn't risk outdriving his headlights. The darkness was complete, and it would be easy to misjudge a curve, doing the dirty work for whoever was behind them.

He slowed for a curve, and their pursuer gained ground.

Gavin's truck was fast, but there was no way to outrun the vehicle gaining on them.

He gripped the wheel tighter as Elliott's voice came through his phone's speaker. "What's going on?"

"Double back." Hayden barked the order. "Someone hit our trail car, and they're gaining fast."

"On the way."

The call ended, but Mia didn't release the phone. She stared at the screen, then turned to look at Ruthie, who slept on, clearly exhausted from her day. It was a small blessing. "Hayden…"

"I'm doing the best I can. I promise." The interior of the truck grew brighter as the car raced up on them. "As soon as we see Elliott's headlights, I'll hit the brakes. We'll confront whoever this is, and we'll make sure they're taken into custody so—"

The vehicle hunting them was only feet away.

Hayden held on to the wheel and lifted his foot from the accelerator. There was no way to avoid what was coming. He just prayed he could hold the truck on the road. "Hang on."

The command was torn by the sound of metal scraping metal as the car tapped his rear bumper, shoving the truck forward.

Hayden fought the wheel as the truck tried to fishtail, barely hanging on as the car dropped back and revved its engine for another run.

Mia covered her mouth with her hands, stifling a scream. Ruthie whimpered in her car seat, but she didn't fully awaken.

While everything in Hayden said to speed toward the help that was speeding toward him, the smarter move was to slow down. If the guy did manage to spin him, it would be easier to maneuver at low speed than at high speed.

His stomach swirled with sick indecision, but he kept his

foot off the gas, letting their speed gradually drop as the car gained again. *Come on, Elliott.* While it felt like hours since he'd called, the reality was it had only been about thirty seconds. It would take Elliott a couple of minutes to arrive.

Minutes that might cost them everything.

The car charged up again, engine roaring. The driver acted as though he was going to pass Hayden and cut him off, but at the last second, he swung his front bumper into the back corner of the truck.

Hayden fought the wheel, but the truck whipped into a sickening spin.

Mia screamed.

Ruthie cried out in fright, ripping his heart in two.

Hayden turned into the skid, but he couldn't regain control. The tires caught loose dirt at the side of the road and traction disappeared.

Mia's scream abruptly shattered as the world exploded.

A force slammed him in the face, blasting him backward, then he slumped forward, the seat belt cutting into his chest. He couldn't see. Couldn't hear. Couldn't tell which way was up. What was happening?

From far away, through the ringing in his ears, he thought he heard a car door slam.

The truck rocked, and Hayden fought for clarity.

Mia. Ruthie.

Someone had run them off the road.

He had to know Mia and Ruthie were okay, had to get them to safety. Forcing himself to breathe, Hayden pressed the seat belt release and looked at Mia, who fought the airbag as she slowly sat up.

She shook her head as though she was covered in cobwebs.

He turned to check on Ruthie.

Her car seat was empty.

The back door hung open.

"Ruthie!" His voice was hoarse, his throat coated with dust from the airbags. Coughing, he sputtered her name again. "Ruthie!"

Turning, he tried to shove his door open but it was stuck. Through the shattered side window, he saw a man shut the back door of a dark sedan, then slide in behind the wheel. The tires screeched as he roared away.

"Ruthie!" Mia screamed, then coughed, her voice jagged. "Ruthie! No!"

Mia screamed again.

Ruthie was gone.

She was dying.

Mia lay curled in a ball on Ruthie's narrow twin bed, her face to the wall and her arms wrapped around her legs. She couldn't remember how she got here. Everything was a blur of sirens and lights and movement.

Just like the night Keith had been murdered.

Her body ached with physical pain and grief. Her memories were a jumbled mess.

All she knew for certain was that the person who had her daughter had torn her heart from her chest and left her a hollow shell.

She pressed her forehead into her knees and dug her fingernails into her arms, desperate to feel something. In all of her worst nightmares, she'd always assumed that if something happened to Ruthie, she'd scream until her lungs collapsed. In reality, there was nothing but heavy, awful, suffocating silence. The weight was too heavy to allow her lungs to expand enough to whimper, let alone release the pain that was killing her.

In the distance, doors opened and closed. The door alarm chimed. Voices murmured in the makeshift command center that had been set up in her kitchen. Hayden was somewhere in the middle of the chaos, knee-deep in the search for Ruthie.

Her one clear memory since that car had struck the rear of their pickup was telling him to leave her alone after he'd helped her upstairs. She'd wanted to be in her own home. She no longer cared if she was safe. She needed to be in Ruthie's room, screaming silent prayers from the center of her being. Prayers that were sheer emotion, void of words.

The loose board in the hall creaked, but Mia didn't bother to acknowledge that someone was upstairs. Hopelessness flowed like thick sludge through her veins. Unless they were coming to say Ruthie was safe, she didn't care.

"Mimi?" The whisper from the doorway was reedy thin with an emotion that matched Mia's own heartbreak.

Mimi. Only one person called her that.

Mia rolled into a sitting position. The sight of her grandmother standing in the doorway with her hands clasped in front of her broke the dam around her emotions. "Noni." The name cracked on a sob.

Immediately, Noni was beside her, wrapping Mia in a familiar embrace. They rocked and cried together, Noni's chin resting on the top of her head. She had no idea how long she sobbed, but by the time the tears stopped, she felt like a limp dishrag.

But she had a clear head, and her lungs no longer felt as though they were clasped in a vise.

With a shuddered breath, Mia sat up and reached for her grandmother's hand. Holding it in both of hers, she sat quietly until she could form words. "I'm scared."

"As you should be." Noni squeezed her hand. "So am I. So is Hayden. So is everyone."

The truth that everyone who loved her daughter was terrified should have incapacitated her, but it did the opposite. It validated her feelings and made her somehow feel inexplicably stronger.

Swallowing the last of her tears, she looked at her Noni. She wasn't alone in this. Everyone who knew and loved her and Ruthie were right here with her, were already in motion to end this nightmare for both of them.

With her free hand, Noni swiped the tears from Mia's cheeks and then from her own. Her brown eyes were warm with compassion, but the deep lines on her face were furrowed with concern. Her shoulder-length gray hair was pulled back with a colorful cloth headband. Although she was nearly eighty, she could still pass for a woman in her sixties. Her days filled with hiking in the mountains and throwing pottery in her art studio kept her strong and full of life.

She squeezed Mia's hand. "I am so sorry this is happening to you, Mimi. You've already been through so much."

"It's not fair."

"No, it's not. It's horrible and unfair and wrong. All of it. If I could carry this weight for you, I would. You know that."

She did. With her parents constantly traveling the world for her father's job, Noni was her constant. Every holiday, every major victory, every crushing defeat, Noni was there. "How did you get here so fast?"

It had been four hours since the moment she'd heard Ruthie's screams from the back seat. At nearly five in the morning, there was no telling what time Noni had hit the road to reach them.

In fact, she'd have had to have left before Ruthie was even taken. "How did you know—"

Noni gave her a soft smile. "I didn't. I came in late last night and stayed at your parents' house, planning to surprise you this morning. I didn't know you'd left to go to Hayden's. I didn't know about anything that was going on."

Mia winced. Everything had happened so quickly that she hadn't told her grandmother anything, hadn't even been able to call her, since her phone was at the house to avoid being tracked. "I'm so sorry. Do Mom and Dad know?"

"I just got off the phone with them. They're doing their best to get here, but being on a cruise ship, it will take some time."

That was true. Given their trip, she hadn't even told them about—

Her stomach squeezed, and she faced her grandmother, holding her hand tighter. "Paige. Noni, Paige is—"

"I know, sweetheart. Hayden filled me in on everything. He called me and told me to come. He had no idea I was only a couple of miles away."

"And, Noni, Blake might be the killer." And the kidnapper.

Noni frowned. "Blake Darby? He's downstairs, and so are his parents. They came with Paige's family."

How? Why? Mia started to jump up, but Noni's grip on her hands stopped her. "Blake is here? Does he have Ruthie? Has he been arrested?"

"Why?" Noni's eyes narrowed.

"He's been off the grid. Vanished. Phone off. No trace of him. I thought… We thought…" Was it all a ruse to make them believe he was innocent?

"He was talking to Hayden when I came upstairs, but he didn't seem to be in any trouble. Hayden seemed to be sympathetic, and Blake seems to be as frantic as the rest of you."

"That doesn't make any sense." Was Blake a friend or the worst foe of all?

"None of this does, and rushing down to accuse Blake of something won't help anything. Hayden and the sheriff are handling it." Noni squeezed Mia's hand. "I'm so glad I listened to my gut and came early. When I was praying for you yesterday morning, something told me to get here quickly."

"Prayer." Mia bit her lip to keep more tears from rolling from her eyes. "I've been praying so hard, but…" She'd prayed for their safety. Had prayed every single day for her baby girl since Paige had asked them to consider adoption. Where had it gotten her?

Nowhere. In fact, she literally had the opposite of everything she'd ever prayed for.

"Don't you go questioning God, Mimi." Noni's voice grew stern, but then her expression softened. "Although if anyone has the right to, I'd say it's you. You've certainly known more than your fair share of heartache, and now this."

"Why?" She'd asked that question so many times since losing Keith, yet she never received an answer.

"We'll likely never know why, but we still have to trust Him. As unfair and horrible as all of this is, we were never promised fair or easy. If life were fair or easy, your grandfather wouldn't have died in Vietnam without ever getting to meet your mother."

"I know." They'd talked about Noni's heartbreak so many times. "You always tell me to pray, but… You knew Jesus for so long before he died that—"

"What?" Noni's head jerked back. "I had no idea who Jesus was when your grandfather died. You know I was steeped in a lifestyle that was nothing less than bohemian. I believed in everything except Jesus. I didn't know anything about Him until your grandfather had been gone for months."

Mia scanned her grandmother's face. "I always thought…

You always talked about how Jesus carried you. How He was there through everything."

"Oh, I was no fan of His, especially not when I was left a widow with a toddler to raise. I'd never disliked another being so much in my life. But then I realized something… When I got angry and frustrated, it wasn't at anyone in the government or on the other side of the world fighting the war. It wasn't at any of the other gods I'd chased around or at the universe. It was at God. And that made me realize that He's real and He exists. So I told Him I knew He was real, but I was good and mad at Him. And after I did that? Mimi, I don't know how to explain this to you, but that's when I felt Him. I screamed and yelled at Him, and when I got it all out, He just kind of…met me with open arms. He didn't bring your grandfather back. He didn't change a thing about my situation, but He let me know He'd walk me through it, and He has. He's walked you through it, too. You've never been alone."

"I know. I've never felt alone, largely because of your story. But I didn't realize you were in the midst of it when you found Him."

"He found me. I sure wasn't looking for Him." Noni smiled gently. "He's here now. I pray with all of my heart Ruthie is safe. I know God's with her, and He's here with us. I used to hold so tight to that verse in Isaiah, and I'm hold-ing to it now."

Mia sniffed. Her grandmother had quoted Isaiah 43:2 to her many times in the past four years. "He's there when we walk in the fire and when we go through the flood." A sob clinched her chest, but she swallowed it. "I'm so tired of the flood."

"I know, baby girl." Noni wrapped a thin arm around Mia's shoulder and pulled her close. "Here's the other thing

I know… You're a woman of action. Of movement. For the past four years, you've been standing still, and it's choking you to death." Mia started to protest, but Noni kept speaking. "I understand the kind of fear that's gripped you. It's real, and I would never diminish that. But I also know that you do best when you're helping others and when the focus is off of you. If you stay up here in this room, you're going to drown in the imaginations of where Ruthie is right now."

Noni was right. As much as she wanted to curl into a huddled mass of pain in the center of Ruthie's mattress, she'd die if she did. She was no help to Ruthie here. "I'm going to go downstairs and see if anybody's hungry or needs help or…" A new fire rose inside of her. Staying in the house wasn't doing anything. She needed to be out searching for her daughter.

Mia rocketed to her feet, dropping Noni's arm from her shoulder. "Or I might join a team that's going out." She'd been trained in search and rescue. If she could put her pain aside, she could help in the hunt for her daughter.

"Now, Mimi." Noni stood. "Let's think this through. I know you need—"

"Mia!" Footsteps pounded on the stairs, then Hayden appeared in the doorway, his hair wild as though he'd continually dragged his hands through it. His eyes were sparking with what might be anger or excitement or both.

Mia stepped toward him, her heart pounding from both his appearance and from the fact that he obviously had news.

He held his hand out to her. "We know who has Ruthie."

FOURTEEN

"That's when I knew something was horribly wrong." Eve Warner sat on the center of Mia's couch, flanked by her parents. Paige's older sister was pale and shaking, and her mother and father appeared to be equally stricken.

Hayden couldn't blame them. Their daughter had been murdered, their biological granddaughter had been kidnapped and now it seemed their son-in-law was the culprit. He couldn't imagine the pain.

He stood near the French doors with his arms crossed, watching the surreal scene unfold in front of him. Nothing about the setting or Mia sitting on a wingback chair beside him was right. Although the family had brought a lawyer and Eve had been walked through her rights, the whole thing was highly unusual. It would be better if this discussion was happening in a different place under more controllable circumstances.

But with Ruthie missing and the clock ticking, they had to move quickly.

When Blake had shown up with his parents a few minutes before Paige's family arrived with a lawyer, everything had kicked into high gear.

Paige's sister, Eve, had been sobbing about her husband Daniel's involvement in Paige's murder and Ruthie's kidnapping. While a detective had talked to her, Hayden had walked into the kitchen with Sheriff Davidson and Blake.

Given that the young man had initially been a suspect, it had been a shock to see him. He'd spilled a quick story that his parents had corroborated and could back up with their doorbell camera video. Blake had been home at the time of Paige's murder, and other than a trip back to Greenville that could be easily checked through credit card records and gas station security camera footage, he'd been with his parents. He'd initially believed that Trent Rhinehart, the husband of Paige's mentor, had something to do with her murder. Apparently, the man had made several unsuccessful passes at Paige over the years.

Blake had followed the Rhineharts back to Greenville when they'd left the Crosby home the day before, but when he'd realized he had no idea what he was looking for, he'd returned home and shared his suspicions with his parents. They'd agreed to call the sheriff this morning, but then news had come that Ruthie was missing.

And now they knew who had her.

Hayden looked around the room, needing a moment to catch his breath. Of all of the suspects they'd listed, Paige's brother-in-law, Daniel Warner, had been low on his list.

"When did you discover all of this?" Sheriff Davidson sat in one of the chairs at an angle to the couch. His fatherly demeanor lent an air of calm to the room, though the tension was thick enough to choke them all.

Eve swallowed audibly. "Daniel went out late yesterday afternoon, and he never came home. He had his johnboat on the trailer when he pulled out. I just assumed he…he…" She leaned against her mother's shoulder, and Sue wrapped her arm around her daughter. "I figured he was grieving Paige and needed…" Eve choked on the words.

Hayden looked away from her sorrow, overwhelmed by his own. According to Eve's first words when she'd walked into the house, Daniel had not only taken Ruthie, he'd killed Paige during an argument. Eve had used a phone app to show the sheriff footage from the video camera in their garage, but Hayden hadn't watched. He'd had his fill of death captured on surveillance cameras.

Elliott had filled him in, having stood over the sheriff's shoulder. In the audio, Daniel had railed at Paige, screaming at her for allowing Ruthie to be adopted "outside of our family." He'd grabbed her, shaken her, screamed at her for "giving away the daughter that should have been" his. When Paige had struggled, he'd shoved her.

She'd stumbled, the back of her head hitting the corner of the johnboat. Elliott said the location and force of the blow against the sharp angle of the boat had likely killed her.

"I never thought he'd take Ruthie. I never thought he'd..." Eve looked across the room at Mia. "I am so sorry. I wish I'd known sooner. I never knew he was feeling all of these things, that he was so angry. That...that he'd do something like this."

Mia stood and squeezed Hayden's hand as she passed. She sat on the table in front of Eve and pulled Paige's sister close.

Hayden watched, wide-eyed. In the midst of her fear and grief, Mia was comforting the wife of the man who'd stolen her daughter? He was pretty sure he was nowhere near that level of selfless.

Eve sobbed into Mia's shoulder. "We've had trouble getting pregnant. We've been through a lot of testing and a couple of rounds of..." She sniffed and sobbed for a long moment. "Last week we found out that Daniel is permanently infertile. He didn't take it well, but I never thought..."

Without warning, Eve sat back, swiping her face. After

a deep breath, she seemed to find resolve. "If he's got the johnboat, he's headed for the waters around Alligator River. He knows that area well and fishes there a lot." She turned to Sheriff Davidson and pulled something from her back pocket. "He didn't take his phone. There's an app on it that lets you mark your favorite fishing spots. I'd start there." She typed something onto the screen and held the device for a moment, staring at it. She hesitated, seeming to consider something before she passed it to the sheriff. "There's more that might… Well, there's also a bunch of texts between him and…Jasmine Jarrett."

Mia gasped. "What?"

At Mia's outburst, Eve flinched, but she recovered quickly. "We met her through a mutual friend, and we'd been talking to her about possibly being a surrogate for us until we found out that Daniel…" Tears welled in her eyes, and her face blushed a deep crimson.

The sheriff spoke as he scrolled through the phone. "Far as I can tell, he began texting her without Eve's knowledge about a week ago. He promised to help Jasmine get revenge on Mia, whatever that means. He's been keeping her updated on Mia's whereabouts, even drove her to Elizabeth City yesterday afternoon."

How had he discovered the connection between Mia and Jasmine?

Not that it mattered. It was clear Daniel had exploited Jasmine's pain to turn her into his puppet.

"Based on one of the early texts, he believed that if Mia was killed, he and Eve would get custody of Ruthie." The sheriff waved over an investigator and handed off the phone. After a low conversation, he stood. "I'll reach out and have ECPD ready to talk to Jasmine as soon as she's able." He turned to a small knot of deputies assembled near the kitchen.

"Let's get Dare and Hyde Counties involved, and federal authorities as well. The wildlife refuge is their jurisdiction, and we'll offer to assist. Call in our volunteer search teams and redirect them to meet us there. I know the sheriff over in Dare will take all the help he can get."

The deputies dispersed, and Mia appeared at Hayden's side. "Your dad still has his skiff, right?"

Odd question. He looked down at her. "He does, but why would…?" The light bulb clicked on. "Mia, no."

Her upturned face held a determination he hadn't seen in a long time. There was no fear. No hesitation. She looked like the "old" Mia, the one who would stand tall against any foe. "Hayden, yes. I am going after my daughter."

He could forbid her, argue with her, try to reason with her, but he'd never win. He recognized the look, and if he was being honest with himself, the ferocity rising inside of her brought him joy, even in this dark time. At least for the moment, she'd successfully wrestled and won against everything that held her back.

He admired her strength. Her love for her daughter. Her willingness to sacrifice for others.

And he loved her for every bit of it and more.

He loved her.

For half a second, he forgot where he was, lost in the dawning of truth. He lifted his hand and trailed a finger down her cheek, pausing at the determined set of her chin.

The instant he looked her in the eye, though, he remembered what was at stake.

He'd take her wherever she wanted to go, would pilot his dad's boat to the ends of the earth if it meant finding Ruthie, reuniting the family he loved more than anything in the world…

And starting his future.

* * *

As the sun rose over the trees along the river at the Alligator River National Wildlife Refuge, the sky glowed in a riot of yellow, red and orange. The trees stood in silhouette against the dawn in the damp, chilled December air. On any other day, it would be a beautiful, praise-God-worthy sight.

Now, it was simply the start of a day on which her daughter was in danger and time to find her was running out. The wildlife refuge consisted of 152,000 acres of wetlands, woodlands and waterways. That meant there were nearly 230 square miles where Daniel Warner could be hiding with her daughter.

And here she was on the water, doing her best to search as many of those miles as she could as the cold dawn broke.

Was she really doing this? For the first time in years, Mia's heart and mind had been clear when she'd forcefully told Hayden that she was joining the search for her daughter. But now?

Now it all felt surreal. She was in that horrible place of suspended reality, where her thoughts felt like they were two steps behind the scene around her.

They skirted the eastern bank of the river, the small outboard motor on the tiny skiff drowned out by the sounds of other, larger boat motors strung out along both banks. Smaller boats like theirs had been deployed in the shallower streams, creeks and canals.

So many boats of so many sizes. Mia couldn't count them all.

If she wasn't so numb, she'd cry. Dozens of first responders were out at dawn on Christmas Eve, braving the unseasonable cold to search for her little girl.

How could she not be out here among them, making the sacrifice herself?

Hayden and a score of other people had urged her to stay at the house and wait for news, but she couldn't. If she wasn't out here being active, she'd wither and die. She needed to be near Ruthie. If Daniel had taken her into the wildlife refuge, then the wildlife refuge was where Mia needed to be.

"You're awfully quiet." Hayden spoke from his seat behind her, at the rear of his father's small skiff, where he was directing their course by turning the boat's motor.

There was too much to say. The thoughts in her head wouldn't sort into conversational pieces. Her daughter was missing. Ruthie's bio-mom was dead. Her bio-uncle was the killer and the kidnapper.

She scanned the bank, searching for the small inlet that would lead them to one of the fishing holes noted on Daniel's app. Apparently, there were a dozen places he frequented.

Hopefully, he'd taken refuge in one of them.

It was always possible he'd led them to believe he was out in the refuge when he was really on a plane to anywhere else in the world.

"Want to talk about it?" Hayden's voice was low, likely a response to the sunrise and the heavy air that hung over the river like fog. Hopefully, it would mute the sounds of the many searchers. If Daniel was alerted to their presence, there was no telling what desperation would drive him to do.

She couldn't think about that, though. "I just can't imagine Daniel doing something like this."

"Neither can I."

A helicopter roared overhead, getting into position to circle wooded areas that would be difficult to traverse on foot. Based on intel handed out at a safety briefing before they'd launched into the river, several more helos were on the way to set up search grids.

They'd find Ruthie. They had to.

Until then, she was left with her whys. "What makes someone steal someone else's child?"

"I don't know." Hayden navigated around a stump that jutted from the riverbank. "Grief? Entitlement? Fear? I can't answer that question."

At least they knew Daniel was seeking a child of his own, not looking to harm anyone, although he'd killed his sister-in-law in a fit of rage. Hopefully, he would be more gentle with a four-year-old.

Mia's hands started to shake. She gripped the sides of the metal skiff, rocking the boat slightly.

Their forward momentum slowed, and Hayden's warm hand rested between her shoulder blades. "Hey. We'll find her."

"We're not exactly quiet out here. All of these boats, helicopters, ATVs..." The sound of engines of all shapes and sizes as they fanned out into the preserve would surely tell Daniel that they'd figured him out. He could hop in that john-boat and go anywhere.

But if he did, surely they'd see him.

Unless he blended in with all of the other boats. It wouldn't be hard to simply join the search and vanish upriver.

But they'd all memorized the photos of Daniel's boat that Eve had provided. They were all on high alert.

God, let it be enough. Let Daniel hear the overwhelming size of our search team and give up.

She had little hope. He was a killer and a kidnapper. What did he have to lose?

"At least Ruthie knows him." Hayden pulled his hand from her back and gave the engine more power. "She won't be afraid of him. And he was apparently dressed as Santa last night. Likely, he's taking great pains to keep her calm so she doesn't alert someone to their presence."

He was just trying to make her feel better. Given his current mental state and sense of desperation, there was no telling what Daniel would do. "Where does he think he's going? Does he plan to live in the swamp with Ruthie forever? What's the plan? He can't—"

A low crackling sound broke through her spinning thoughts. From the walkie-talkie on Hayden's belt, Sheriff Davidson's voice rasped into the air. "Got word from Dare County. Daniel's truck was found on Buffalo City Road near the kayak launch. No boat on the trailer."

"That's not far from here." Hayden let the small skiff drift in shallow water near the bank, where a creek dipped into the trees and headed back toward the interior of the wetlands. He pulled the radio from his hip and spoke into it. "We've got several inlets over here. We'll take the one at…" He checked his GPS and read off the coordinates.

The sheriff relayed the coordinates, then ordered several other teams to head their way, both to search other waterways and to provide backup.

Hayden clipped the radio back onto his belt, then turned the craft slowly into the narrow creek that opened up into one of the kayak paddling trails.

Mia leaned forward. Somewhere in the shadows between the trees, her daughter was being held captive. She refused to let herself believe in anything but a successful outcome.

But, still…

Lord, let us find her before it's too late.

FIFTEEN

Hayden tried to keep an eye on the creek in front of him and also on Mia, who was strangely calm and quiet. Searchers had taken to land, water and sky to find Ruthie. Members of his Trinity team had taken off on foot, joining a search party that was working their way through the woods nearby. They had to succeed. If they didn't...

He didn't want to think about life if they didn't.

He navigated around a stump in the creek that wound away from the river. The narrow, shallow channel was more suited to a canoe than a skiff, though recent rains were helping them out. The app on Daniel's phone listed a site along one of the creeks near here as a place where Daniel liked to fish, so it was an area he was familiar with and might be comfortable hiding in.

But Mia...

When she'd informed him she was heading out on the search, he'd been so proud of her. But he'd also expected her to buckle under the weight of Ruthie's disappearance, especially after her grandmother had repeatedly suggested she stay at the house to wait for news.

He was kind of ashamed of those thoughts. How many times had he told Mia he believed she was stronger than she thought she was? Now he was the one doubting she could handle the stress.

A kidnapped child was an extraordinary amount of pressure, though, the kind that could break even someone who wasn't struggling with PTSD the way Mia was.

Still, he knew from experience in both himself and those he'd served with that PTSD was a strange illness. It affected everyone differently, driving some to abuse substances, some to chase adrenaline highs and others to withdraw inside of themselves. He'd seen fellow soldiers completely change personalities, doing things they'd never dreamed they'd do. He'd seen others internalize their pain until they imploded.

And then there was Mia. In the moments when life was easy, fear hunted her and threatened to drive her to the ground. But when the danger was real and the threat was in her face? It was as though reality was less terrifying than the monsters that chased her thoughts.

He powered back the small motor on his dad's little fishing skiff as they eased deeper into the trees. With the sun just over the horizon, the wooded area around them still hung heavy with shadows where danger could hide. It would be easy to glide right past Ruthie and Daniel without ever seeing them.

As they made their way farther, the sounds of the other boats faded into distant mosquitoes, background noise that seemed to buzz through his ever-racing thoughts and prayers for Ruthie's safety.

The deeper the silence grew, the more he wanted to shatter it with a bloodcurdling scream.

Instead he reached out to Mia. "It's too quiet. Talk to me." If only she knew how much he needed to hear her voice. It had been that way for years—how was he just now seeing it?

How was he just now realizing that he'd fallen in love

with her? He couldn't pinpoint the moment it had happened, and he couldn't have picked a worse time to uncover those emotions.

She looked over her shoulder at him, her ponytail falling down her back. "I'm doing a lot of praying, but I've been doing it quietly because I'm not good at doing it out loud."

"How are you holding up?"

Her chin tipped toward the ever-brightening tree canopy above them. "Numb. Scared. Overwhelmed. Lost. All of the things. I'm probably not doing as badly as I'd be doing if I was sitting in the house waiting for the phone to ring." She sniffed. "It's still hard. With me, it's tough to know what's normal and what's my brain going into overdrive."

It couldn't be easy to be trapped in her own mind. It wasn't easy to be in his own head most of the time.

He felt as though the engine in his brain had been stuck in high gear for years, but he'd become so used to it that he hadn't noticed. Now the roaring was about to swamp him.

But this wasn't about him. "I think feeling all of those things you said is normal right now. And, Mia? Just because your feelings are different than other people's, that doesn't mean you aren't normal. After all you've been through, you'd be abnormal if you weren't overwhelmed. I'd be worried about you if the world *didn't* scare you more than it scares other people."

Slowly, she tilted her head down. For a long time, she stared ahead of them, where the water broadened as they neared one of the larger creeks that ran parallel to the river. Ahead, the air seemed brighter where the trees thinned.

Finally, Mia braced her hands on the sides of the skiff and turned to look at him, rocking the small boat gently. Tears stood in her eyes. "You're right. My baby girl is missing. It's normal to be afraid. My husband was murdered, and I watched him bleed out in front of me while our baby was in her carrier beside him. Who's to judge what a normal reaction to that is? All this time…" Her gaze met his and held on. She blinked, and tears glistened down her cheeks. "All this time, I've been measuring my life against everyone else's. Everyone else hasn't been through what I've been through." She nodded, her ponytail bobbing as though it could express her resolve. "I have to heal in my own way. Who's to say what's *normal* when nothing about this is normal?" Looking away from him, she turned around as though she'd settled something in her heart.

He'd definitely settled some things in his. Watching the light dawn in her eyes, he'd felt his feelings settle into place, had heard Elliott's words all over again. Their lives weren't dictated by how anyone else lived. Everyone had their own story. He'd been her friend for years. Had been Keith's friend even longer. They were part of each other's histories.

There was a Psalm in the Bible somewhere that said God had written his days in a book before he was ever born. If that was the case, then He knew how it all started, how it continued and how it ended.

Keith's book had a start, a middle and an end. He'd lived his life fully, serving those around him and loving his wife and daughter for as long as he'd been able. There was no doubt in Hayden's mind that, given Keith's actions and his commitment to Jesus, he'd gone to be with Him when he died.

But Mia's book was still being written. So was his own. So was Ruthie's. One person's book being closed didn't mean that all of the other books simply ended. God continued writing chapters.

And maybe their chapters blended into a whole new book. Maybe there was a sequel.

A spiderweb brushed his forehead as they passed between two tree limbs. Hayden shuddered and swiped at the sticky threads. It felt like a hundred spiders skittered across his skin, but he shook off the sensation along with his shiny new thoughts about Mia.

Right now, finding Ruthie was the most important thing. They couldn't afford any distractions.

He scanned the trees and the water, throttling the boat's motor back, then shutting it off as they reached the wider creek. He didn't need to roar out of the trees with the engine humming. The sound would carry up and down the open stretch of water for a good distance. If Daniel was nearby, the last thing they wanted to do was alert him to their presence.

Hayden grabbed a low-hanging branch and held on, anchoring them against the gentle current that tried to push them back toward the river.

The morning air was quiet. The sound of the other boats on the river and in the various waterways had faded as they drifted deeper into the pocosin wetlands.

Actually...

He scooted off the small bench seat onto his knees in the damp bottom of the boat and leaned closer to Mia so he could whisper. "It's too quiet."

She held her breath, seeming to listen before she nodded. "No birds."

She had picked up on what he'd noticed. Not only were the birds in the nearby trees silent, but they were silent along the creek as well.

It could be because of their presence or because of the cold air, but even in the winter the birds in the area tended to greet the sunrise.

They weren't the only ones out here.

Had other searchers stumbled into their grid? Or was Daniel nearby with Ruthie?

Hayden reached for his radio, then hesitated. He couldn't call others away from their search areas on a hunch. To do so might mean they missed Ruthie completely and allowed Daniel to escape.

He'd already let one person who'd harmed the people he loved escape. He wasn't about to let that happen again.

Suddenly, Mia stiffened. She held up her hand before Hayden could speak and leaned forward, turning her right ear toward the creek.

As much as he wanted to ask what she'd heard, he kept his mouth shut, not wanting to cover another sound.

But then it came again, clearer.

"Now, Uncle Daniel!" It was Ruthie's voice.

And she was angry.

Mia nearly choked on her daughter's name. It rushed into her throat, begging to cry out.

"I want to go home!" The shout bounced off the trees and pierced her heart.

Only Hayden's hand on her shoulder kept her from leaping from the skiff into the shallow creek to rush through the water toward the distant sound of her daughter's ire.

Ruthie wasn't scared, but she was angry. There was no telling how long Daniel would deal with a temper tantrum before he snapped like he had with Paige.

Mia whimpered and struggled, and Hayden drew her back against his chest, covering her mouth gently with his hand. "Shh. I know. I know."

Every muscle in her body shook with tension and the screaming desire to charge forward. Her daughter was nearby. The longer they waited, the more likely it was that Daniel would pack her up and flee deeper into the wildlife preserve.

She had to go. Had to get to her daughter. Had to rescue her.

She could not be too late again. She could not lose her daughter because she arrived on the scene after the damage was done.

She couldn't.

Tears streamed down her cheeks as she struggled, the drops running between Hayden's fingers where his hand covered her mouth.

He continued to whisper words she couldn't quite make out, but they rose and fell with a cadence she recognized as his prayers. His chest pressed against her back, and his heartbeat raced along at what felt like the same speed as hers.

Hayden was as terrified as she was. He wanted to race in to snatch Ruthie back to them as much as she did.

He loved her daughter as much as she did. He would do the right thing.

She took a shuddered breath in through her nose, then exhaled slowly, forcing herself to relax.

The moment she did, Hayden slipped his hand from her mouth, but he didn't pull away from her. Instead, he whispered, "I'm going to text our coordinates to the sheriff." He moved away and secured the boat to a tree branch with a rope. As he shifted forward in the small craft, there was a soft click. He'd shut off his radio, not wanting to risk it going off and alerting Daniel to their location.

"Ruthie. Get in the boat." Daniel's shout knifed through the trees. They had to hurry. He was loading up to move. There was no doubt he'd heard the helicopters and the boats.

It was possible he had a police scanner, and although they'd been careful about communications, he'd still be able to deduce that they'd figured out his location.

How did he expect to escape? The area was crawling with boats and with searchers on foot and in the air. Helicopters would easily track him.

But if he took off deeper into the preserve before they made contact, he could disappear once again.

"I want to go home. I want Mommy." Ruthie's anger carried, and her foot stomp was clear in Mia's mind, even if it wasn't visible in her sight.

Her heart shredded at her daughter's demands. Ruthie might be angry, but she was also scared. She needed her mother. Mia's breath stuttered, and she instinctively leaned forward to jump into the water.

She had to get to her little girl.

Hayden grabbed a fistful of her sweatshirt and pulled her to him. "Backup is on the way."

"If he gets her into a boat or he gets cornered…" There was no telling what Daniel would do if he was backed into a situation he couldn't get out of. He might hurt Ruthie. He was likely desperate enough to do anything at this point. "We can't wait."

"If you promise me you'll stay right here, I'll go see what we're dealing with." Hayden turned her to face him, gripping her shoulders to force her to look him in the eye. "Promise."

She nodded. While her impulses drove her to her daughter, her training and instincts planted her where she was. They couldn't go in without intel. That would only get one of them hurt, possibly Ruthie.

She had to think like a soldier. Like a law enforcement officer. Not like a mother.

Even if it ripped her insides apart.

When she nodded, Hayden slid his hand down to hers, then lifted her hand and wrapped her fingers around the branch he'd been holding. "Stay here." He laid his radio and cell phone on the bench seat, scanned her face, then grabbed the back of her neck and pressed a quick kiss to her lips before he turned away, gripping the side of the skiff. "Hold it steady."

Mia grabbed the rough branch with both hands, her mind and heart reeling. Her daughter. Hayden. The danger. That kiss. The other kiss. Her twisting, turning feelings.

It was too much.

The small boat rocked as Hayden stepped over the side into water that came just over his knees. Carefully, he made his way up the stream, avoiding the super-saturated ground along the bank that would suck his feet down and lock him into place.

He moved achingly slow, obviously not wanting to make too much noise as he waded closer to the larger creek. Once he reached the outlet, there would be no cover, and he had no way of knowing exactly where Daniel and Ruthie were or if Daniel was watching.

One move made too quickly could end everything.

Mia wanted to curl into a ball in the skiff. To press her face against the water puddled in the flat bottom of the metal boat, close her eyes and pretend that none of this was happening. Maybe she'd open her eyes to a different world, where she was at home in her own bed, with Ruthie safely tucked in down the hall.

Instead, her eyes dried out from not blinking as she watched Hayden's slow progress. If she looked away or let her attention lag, something horrible might happen to him.

She should pray, but the only prayers she could muster were jumbled silent screams from her heart.

That verse about God understanding even when she didn't have words had better be true.

Hayden stopped and grabbed the trunk of a tree that grew out of the water. He edged closer to the trunk, using the tree as a shield. Pressing as tightly as he could against the bark, he eased forward to look around the tree.

He jerked back, then looked directly at Mia. Deliberately raising his arm, he extended his left index finger, pointing in the direction he'd been looking, his thumb aimed at the ground.

It was a military hand signal. *Enemy in sight.*

Mia nearly collapsed into the bottom of the boat. Ruthie really was nearby, and Daniel had her. She wasn't sure whether to feel relief or panic, but she managed to lift a thumb in acknowledgment.

With grim determination on his face, Hayden lifted his arm again, this time bending his elbow and making a fist.

Freeze.

He expected her to stay in place.

There was no way she was going to give him a thumbs-up to that. If he thought she was going to stay here while he—

He shifted signals, holding his hand to his ear like a telephone.

Mia scrambled for the radio, then stopped. If Hayden wasn't speaking, then she didn't dare risk being heard. Following his earlier lead, she grabbed his cell phone and unlocked it using Ruthie's birthday, then texted Sheriff Davidson. Located Ruthie and Daniel at our last location.

The reply came quickly. Is he armed?

She had no idea.

Oh, Lord, don't let him be armed. She couldn't bear it if

her daughter was being held captive at gunpoint. Guns had done enough damage to her life already.

She sent her answer. Don't know.

Headed your way on foot and by water. Don't engage unless necessary.

Clearly they hoped to rescue Ruthie by appearing in front of Daniel with overwhelming force.

Mia settled the phone onto the bench and lifted her hands above her head, crossing her wrists. *Remain in place.*

Hayden acknowledged with a raised thumb, then peeked around the tree, his hand at his hip.

Mia's spine stiffened. He wouldn't do that if Daniel was unarmed.

If she sat here any longer, she'd fly into pieces. Already, her heart was pounding and her skin was heating. Her mind raced, and her muscles ached to move. She was headed for a full-blown panic attack that would blow their cover if she didn't get moving.

This wasn't a mission, and Hayden wasn't her commanding officer. This was her daughter's life at stake, and she wasn't going to let him call the shots, even if his calls made sense.

She grabbed the branch above her head to steady herself, then slipped one leg over the side and stepped into the water.

Her running shoes sank into mud, but she moved slowly and deliberately through the water. She was halfway to Hayden, who glared at her with concern and anger, before she realized she'd left the radio and his cell phone behind.

She'd also misjudged how cold the water was. Her legs were freezing, and the shakes started almost instantly. Whether they were from cold or fear, she couldn't say, but she didn't dare stop moving.

She reached Hayden's side, and he glared in a way that made her glad she couldn't read his mind.

"What do you see?" She leaned against him and whispered directly into his ear.

He turned away, took a deep breath, then turned back to her. "Tent. Boat. Daniel. Ruthie's fine but not happy."

As if to punctuate his words, Ruthie cried out again. "Uncle Daniel! Take me home so Santa can find me!"

"Ruthie! Knock it off!" Daniel's voice roared across the space.

Mia swallowed a cry, but not fast enough. Her daughter's name was halfway out of her mouth before she clamped down on her shout.

"Mommy!" Ruthie's frantic voice cut through the morning, followed by a series of curses from Daniel.

They had no choice but to move.

Hayden stepped from cover, his hand on his hip, facing the right. "Daniel, you need to give up. Hand Ruthie over. There are reinforcements—" He jerked and reached for his hip, but before he could grab his gun, a shot cracked. Hayden grabbed at his face, stepped backward and stumbled, disappearing beneath the waist-deep water.

Mia's scream blended with her daughter's on the echo of the gunshot.

SIXTEEN

"No!" Mia's scream echoed off the trees. She lurched forward, her knees giving way, and dropped into water up to her stomach. Icy shivers ran through her.

Not again. Not again. Not again.

Keith.

Hayden.

Gunshots.

Death.

"No!" The word ripped from her throat, tearing at her vocal cords. She would not, could not, lose another man she loved. Not like this. Not to—

"Mommy!" Ruthie's cry was followed by a splash.

"Ruthie. Get back here!" Daniel's yell was hot with fury. The same fury that had killed Paige.

Mia scrambled to her feet, the need to rescue her daughter breaking through the toxic fog of fear, shock and grief.

Ruthie needed her. That night at the Double R Convenience Store, Mia had frozen at the sight of Keith's body, leaving her daughter helpless in her car seat while someone else rushed in to save her.

Not this time.

Her daughter was in danger, and she would not fail her again. It was up to her, and with Hayden…

Swallowing a whimper, Mia stepped forward as the cold water on her body seemed to freeze in the icy air. If she didn't get to Ruthie quickly, her daughter would freeze in the water. She had no doubt the splash had been Ruthie diving in and rushing toward the sound of her mother's voice.

Mia waded the remaining few feet to the opening in the canal, heedless of Daniel's presence and unable to force herself to look toward where Hayden had vanished. *Dear Lord...* There were no other words. If she considered what had happened, she'd drop in her tracks.

A few bubbles surfaced where he'd vanished, and their trail seemed to move against the current. Was he hurt? Was he swimming to safety? How could she be facing this again?

She dragged her gaze to her daughter, praying for Hayden, for Ruthie, for herself.

Ruthie. She had to focus on Ruthie.

Clear of the overhanging trees, the sky above was bright with morning's light, though shadows overhung the creek and its banks.

On the other side of the wide creek, about forty feet away, Daniel had beached his johnboat. A small tent stood on the bank, and Daniel was splashing into the water, headed straight for her.

Six or so feet from the bank, Ruthie was wading into ever deeper water, nearly up to her neck already. Her hazel eyes locked on to her mother's. "M-M-Mommy!" The cry came through chattering teeth.

"Ruthie!" Only sheer determination kept Mia from collapsing with both fear and relief. Her daughter was safe at this very second, but submerged in frigid water with Daniel on her heels, that could change at any moment.

Daniel froze when he was knee-deep in the water, his expression registering shock at Mia's appearance. He was only a few feet away from Ruthie.

His hands were empty. He must have dropped the gun somewhere in his rush to reach Ruthie. Sure enough, he turned from Mia toward his boat, then back again. "Mia. You have no part in this. Don't make me hurt you."

She ignored him. Her daughter was her only priority. Let Daniel roar. She needed to get Ruthie back to the skiff. Back to where Hayden had disappeared.

Or she had to stall Daniel long enough for the cavalry to arrive.

Mia focused on her daughter, who was up to her neck as she tried to wade to her mother. Mia couldn't tell her to go back to shore, because Daniel was frozen in indecision near the bank. "Ruthie. You can get to me. I'll meet you in the middle." Ruthie had been swimming from the moment she could float. "It's too deep to walk. Swim."

"Cold." Even from this distance, it was clear that Ruthie's lips were turning blue. The greatest danger to her daughter right now wasn't Daniel. It was nature itself.

"I know, baby." They should have brought blankets, extra coats, something. Hopefully, the sheriff and his team had thought ahead. "Come to Mommy." She plowed through water that dragged her back. She was freezing where her wet skin met the air. Shivering. Weakening.

"Stay away from my daughter!" Daniel shouted and stepped deeper into the water. "I'm taking Ruthie where she'll be safe. Paige and Blake never should have—"

"I w-want to go h-home." Ruthie was close. Just out of arm's reach.

Mia reached over the water. "Come on, little fish." Her fingers brushed her daughter's, then she clasped Ruthie's cold wrist and pulled her into her arms, snuggling her to her chest. "It's okay, baby. Mommy's got you. We're going home. We're going to have hot chocolate and see Noni." She had to get back into cover and toward the river before Daniel could recover and react.

She had to get back to Hayden. Was he hurt? Alive? Was he...

There was no sign of him.

She turned to slog to the creek and the skiff, but splashing from Daniel's direction stopped her. Before she could look to see what he was doing, a gunshot cracked, and dead leaves rained down from above.

Ruthie cried out and tightened her grip around Mia's neck.

Mia froze. Gunshots. Daniel knew her trauma, her pain, her fear. Mia whimpered.

"Don't make me shoot you in the back, Mia." His voice was hard. "I've got nothing to lose." His voice cracked, then strengthened again. "Paige was an accident, but Hayden wasn't. If it means I take Ruthie and start a life with the daughter I deserve, the one Eve and I should have adopted, then I will do whatever it takes to leave with her."

Everything she feared most swirled around her. Ruthie in danger. The thought of leaving Ruthie as an orphan. Someone she loved injured or dead.

Injured or dead.

She stared at the spot where Hayden had been shot, where he'd disappeared into the water. She'd seen enough drowning victims to know that something should be visible, especially in water this shallow. His coat. His arm. Something.

Hope surged. Maybe she'd been wrong. Maybe Hayden was alive.

Then where was he?

In the distance, the low hum of boat motors surged.

Help was on the way, but would it be in time?

She looked over her shoulder, where Daniel aimed a double-barreled shotgun in her direction.

A shotgun. Two shells. Unless he'd reloaded, and she was fairly certain there hadn't been time, then he had no more ammo in the weapon.

A shotgun also meant whatever Daniel had fired at Hayden had likely been shells filled with some sort of shot. From that distance, the damage would have been minimal. So where was he?

Behind her, a series of splashes indicated that Daniel was in pursuit. He'd be faster than her with Ruthie in her arms. He'd catch them. He'd drown her. He'd take Ruthie.

Where was Hayden? Would help arrive before it was too late?

She looked over her shoulder, and Daniel was gaining, cutting through the water faster than she ever could. She shivered as Ruthie shuddered.

She tried to gauge the distance to the skiff, then looked back again. Daniel was only twenty feet away. So close. So—

Something splashed between her and the skiff. She collided with something hard. A tree trunk. A—

An arm, dripping water from a heavy black work coat, wrapped around her and Ruthie, pulling them close and then moving them aside.

With water pouring from his hair and his coat and blood mixing with the water on his face, Hayden lifted his hand, his pistol aimed squarely at Daniel. "Stop now." He stepped in front of Ruthie and Mia. "It's over, Daniel."

With a sob, Mia leaned forward. She rested her chin on her daughter's shivering head and her forehead against the back of Hayden's soaking wet jacket, cradling Ruthie between them.

Behind her, shouts indicated that several other search teams were almost upon them.

It was over.

He'd better be right about Daniel not reloading.

Hayden held the pistol level, aimed at Daniel's center mass. The last thing he wanted to do was pull the trigger.

If he was right, he shouldn't have to.

Although Daniel stood about twenty feet away with the shotgun aimed at them, he didn't pull the trigger. He merely glared at Hayden as though he wished that first shot had killed him.

Hayden didn't want to consider how Mia must have felt in those long moments as he had maneuvered into position to end this fight. His heart had ached for her, his pulse throbbing in the small wounds that dotted his face and neck from the birdshot.

Keith had to be on her mind. She had to be reliving a nightmare. He'd wanted to cry out to her, to let her know he was safe, but then Daniel would have known as well.

He'd have had time to reload.

If Hayden was right, Daniel had no ammo. He had fired once at Hayden and once at the sky. That shotgun only held two shells. He hadn't seen Daniel reload, but it had also taken him some time to get from where he'd taken a dive under the shallow water to where he'd surfaced in the shadows.

Nothing else had gone to plan. Not getting peppered in the face with birdshot. Not surfacing to find that Mia had surged forward to confront Daniel unarmed.

She trembled against his back, shaking Ruthie's head against his shoulder blade. He was cold and numb, and surely they were, too, but he wasn't about to let Daniel Warner escape. As boat motors drew closer, he held his ground.

Red-faced and with a look harsh enough to drop a man in his tracks, Daniel tossed the shotgun into the water, then raised his hands.

At the same time, a helicopter roared overhead and hovered, stirring the trees and scattering dead leaves over water that whipped into small waves.

Daniel looked up, then ducked his head against the onslaught of rotor wash. There was nothing the aircraft could do, and he likely realized that. It couldn't land. It could only hover, letting the approaching water teams know their exact location.

Hayden reached behind his back and pushed Mia and Ruthie away. "Go. Get to cover. Now."

Mia wrapped an arm around his waist, her grip tight. No doubt she was overwhelmed and panicked.

Daniel saw his opportunity. He bolted toward the boat he'd beached on the narrow bank. The chances of him getting away were small, but the likelihood that he had another weapon stashed on the boat was large. If he reached it, it could lead to a firefight that endangered Ruthie, Mia and the searchers who had nearly reached them.

Hayden ripped Mia's hand from his waist, holstered his pistol and pushed through the water, desperate to reach Daniel before he reached the boat. Swimming would be faster, but the water was too shallow.

He had to get to Daniel. He didn't want a gun battle. Didn't want to pull the trigger. Didn't want Eve and the rest of Paige's family to live with Daniel's death the way Mia and he had to live with Keith's.

Just as Daniel reached the stern of the boat, Hayden pushed forward with one final lunge, knocking them both sideways into the knee-deep water.

Daniel rolled, seeking the advantage, but Hayden was

faster. He came to his feet first and was already swiping water from his eyes. He eased around, putting himself between Daniel and the boat.

Scrambling to his feet with water dripping from his dark hair, Daniel backed a few feet away, eyeing first the boat, then Hayden, as though he was calculating his next move. He had to know he had a better chance of escape if he fled on foot deeper into the preserve, but his tenacious desire to get to the boat clarified Hayden's suspicions that he had a second weapon on board.

Gun or knife, it didn't matter. Hayden wasn't letting him get past. His body ached and his face burned, but he held his ground.

The fear in Daniel's eyes was more frightening than any hatred could have been. The man knew he was backed into a corner, and corners made people desperate.

Without warning, Daniel whirled and fled onto the bank, stumbling toward the woods.

Elliott and Rebecca stepped out of the shadows, accompanied by two deputies who had their hands on their holsters.

Elliott offered a trademark grin. "Somebody call for the cavalry?"

Hayden could only nod, too cold to speak. He'd never been happier to see his teammates.

To the left, a boat appeared from farther up the wide, shallow creek, piloted by another deputy.

Hayden reached up and grabbed the side of the johnboat. It truly was over this time. His adrenaline ebbed, leaving him weak and shaky. The cold and the pain finally registered, and he sank to his knees in chilly water. Ruthie and Mia were safe. The threat was gone.

He turned as quickly as he could as the deputies took Daniel into custody, searching for Mia and Ruthie, but they were nowhere to be found. One of the skiffs that had entered from the direction of the river was powering away, carrying the woman he loved and the kid he adored to safety.

Without him.

SEVENTEEN

Her home was safe once again.

Mia sat in the rocking chair in Ruthie's room and watched the rise and fall of her daughter's chest as she slept beneath the orange-and-pink-striped quilt. Ruthie's hair was a mass of tangles on the bright orange pillow, and she snuggled Penelope close. The doll had been left in Hayden's truck, but Elliott had proved to be the hero. He'd spotted Penelope in the wreckage and tucked the doll away in his own truck. Penelope had been waiting on Ruthie's bed when they came home from their short trip to the hospital ER, where they'd been evaluated for hypothermia and checked for other injuries before being sent home with a "prescription" for warm pj's, hot soup and a long rest.

Ruthie had been happier to see Penelope than she had been to see her mother. Almost.

Mia smiled. That was fine. Hopefully it was an indicator that she'd wouldn't suffer any lasting effects from her ordeal. A chat with a kind investigator had revealed that Daniel had not harmed Ruthie. She had, in fact, believed it was a grand adventure in search of Santa Claus, and had been more angry about not being allowed to go home than she had been afraid of what was happening. Only at the end, when they'd arrived to rescue her, had Ruthie begun to realize something was wrong.

There was hardship ahead of her, though. They had yet to tell her about Paige's death. Mia dreaded the moment when the truth was spoken.

For now, she was content to sit and rock and to watch Ruthie sleep, knowing that both Daniel and Jasmine were in custody.

Life would be good…if only Hayden would reach out to her.

The last time she'd seen him, he'd been standing in the water after help arrived. At that point, Gavin and Kelsie had hauled her and Ruthie away from the scene, rushing them to the river where a larger boat waited with blankets and dry clothes to combat the effects of cold water and colder air. They hadn't seen Hayden at the ER, nor had he called since.

Mia tapped her fingers on her knee. She had heard no updates. He'd been shot with birdshot from a distance, which shouldn't be too damaging, but still…

He'd been shot.

The truth sent a tremor through her, one she'd been holding back since the blast. Had Daniel been armed with a pistol or a rifle instead of a shotgun…

Mia stood so suddenly that the world tilted. She breathed deeply, trying to beat back vertigo and the panic attack that threatened to overwhelm her.

"He's okay." The low, deep voice from the doorway whirled her around, slamming the brakes on her fear.

Elliott held up his hands as if to show he was unarmed. The man who typically looked unflappable had a bit of a sheepish pink to his complexion, probably because he had invaded what he perceived to be "girl territory."

It was almost enough to make Mia smile.

He pointed toward the stairs and turned in that direction.

"I know it's going to take a lot to get you away from your daughter, but can I talk to you?" When Mia's smile faded, Elliott shook his head. "Hey, I already told you Hayden's okay. So is everybody else. This is just a talk." Without waiting to see if she complied, he walked away.

A talk with Hayden's boss? A man who was clearly used to giving orders that were followed without question?

Since both the army and the sheriff's department had conditioned her to follow orders…

With one last glance at her daughter, Mia stepped out, pulling the door closed behind her. Knowing Ruthie, she'd nap until dinner. The kid slept like a champ.

In the den, Elliott was studying the Christmas tree when Mia walked in. He turned, shoving his hands into his pockets beneath his gray flannel shirt. "You go all out for Christmas?"

Mia wrapped her arms around her stomach and sat on the edge of the couch. The house was quiet. Her grandmother had run to the grocery store for dinner, the search teams had departed, and the Trinity team had scattered except for Elliott and Kelsie, who was nowhere to be seen. "It's for Ruthie. I'm not a fan, but she deserves the cheer. It seems like bad always happens at Christmas. That's when…" She looked toward the French doors, where the open blinds revealed Christmas Eve afternoon sunlight sparkling on the river. "Now this."

"You're a good mom."

She shrugged. "I try." When she looked at Elliott, he was still watching her. "Have you heard any more about what's going to happen to Daniel and Jasmine?"

"You and I both know any real answers will be slow in coming, but Daniel's revealed that he met Jasmine when they were looking for a surrogate, and it came out pretty quickly who you were and that Jasmine had some, well, hard feelings against you."

That was a gross understatement.

Elliott brushed a tree branch. "He'd never been happy with Paige about the way the adoption went, and meeting Jasmine was the match to that gasoline. His initial plan was to have Jasmine panic you into fleeing the café to make you vulnerable to attack, but that was obviously derailed. All of that was in the works days before his altercation with Paige, and once she was dead, he had no choice but to go all-in on getting Ruthie by any means necessary. With a confession like that, both of them are going to jail."

Barring a plea deal of some sort, Daniel's sentence could be for life. That poor family had been through far too much. It hurt her heart to think of it. When she looked up, Elliott was still watching her. "Did you have something else you wanted to say?"

"Probably not my place to say it, but I'm going to anyway." His grin lit brown eyes that were warmer than she'd initially thought. "I've never been one who kept my nose out of other people's business when I saw something that needed to be fixed."

Mia's forehead wrinkled. "Okay?"

Curling one side of his mouth, Elliott looked at the fireplace. "PTSD is a cruel companion, and it's something some of us have to live with. We learn to cope."

"It forces us into a new normal." Mia eyed Hayden's boss. Clearly, he was fighting his own battles. "I've started figuring that out the past couple of days."

"Good. Just know that having a new normal doesn't mean we stop fighting it or looking for ways to get better. It doesn't mean we stop living." Elliott finally looked at her. "I just want you to know I'm going to commit Trinity Investigations to this second look at what happened to your husband. We're going to find answers for you."

Gratitude warmed her. Someone outside of her small circle was fighting to bring Keith's killer to justice. "That means a lot. Thank you."

"And about that…" Elliott shifted from one foot to the other.

"Yes?" It was interesting to see him ill at ease. He was like a lost little boy.

Elliott lifted a slight smile, as though he'd read her thoughts. "I'm going to tell you something I said to Hayden the other night. You're still alive. So is he. And I think the two of you need to have an honest conversation about—"

"You butting into my business, *boss*?"

Mia jumped up and turned toward the kitchen door.

Hayden stood there, a smile belying the tone of his voice.

"Hayden." He was here. Alive and walking. His face and neck were peppered with small cuts and a couple of bandages. His hair was a mess, and his face was drawn with exhaustion.

He'd never looked better.

She'd never loved him more.

He flicked a glance at her, then looked at Elliott. "I think Kelsie needs some help downstairs with the grill. She said something about hot dogs."

"Roger that, McGrath."

Mia didn't see Elliott leave, though she heard the front door close behind him. Her entire focus was on Hayden.

He was right, though. They had some talking to do, because the biggest thing she'd learned was something she'd known for months but had refused to acknowledge.

She loved Hayden. It was possible to honor Keith's memory while loving Hayden. She needed to be honest about her feelings, whether he reciprocated them or not, because she couldn't continue with the status quo. Not when her feelings had become very real and very obvious. Not when she wanted to spend the rest of her life with her best friend.

She had no idea where to start. "Are you okay?"

He stepped closer, slowly and deliberately. "Spent a couple of hours getting stitches and some IV antibiotics. Probably have a few scars. It'll be okay, though, if—" He reached the back of the couch across from her and stopped.

He was only a few feet away. She could reach out and touch him, but a sudden fear washed through her.

Not the kind of fear that had paralyzed her since Keith's death. This was different. She saw a new future laid out in front of her, one that involved her and Hayden and Ruthie as a family, but she was terrified he might not want the same.

She cleared her throat. "Ruthie is good. She's taking a nap. Noni went to get those hot dogs, and we're going to have a nontraditional Christmas Eve din—"

"I don't want to talk about dinner." His voice was deep and quiet, the tone one she'd never heard before.

It hit her spine and ran straight down to her toes, robbing her knees of strength. "What do you want to talk about?" The words were a whisper. Her breath was gone. Her heart was racing.

But this was no panic attack.

This was the exact opposite. It was...

It was everything.

Hayden extended his hands across the back of the couch. "Writing a new chapter."

Was he saying...? Mia rested her hands in his. His fingers were warm and slipped between hers like missing puzzle pieces.

He tugged gently, and she knelt on the couch, unwilling to take the time to walk all the way around it. All she wanted was to be in the protection of his arms. To know he was safe and she was, too…and that they both wanted the same things.

He slid his hands up her arms to her shoulders, then pulled her to him and wrapped his arms around her waist with the back of the couch between them. He nuzzled her hair until his lips were soft against her ear. "You know, don't you?"

"Know what?" Oh, she did, but she wanted to hear him say it.

"That I love you. Everything about you, Mia Galloway." He pulled away and slid his arms from her waist, cupping her cheeks in his palms. "The way you love Ruthie. The way you're always there when I need you. The way you need me. The way you're the bravest person I know. The way you honor Keith and yet…"

"And yet I love you." She wrapped her arms around his neck and pulled him close, kissing him in a way that said all of the things she couldn't. Giving her heart to the man God had given her for this moment, for this time, for as long as He allowed them to have.

She was going to grasp life again. To grasp joy again. To continue fighting…with Hayden by her side.

They could do this. Together.

She had a deeply rooted feeling that Keith would want them to take care of each other when he couldn't. That God had known the end from the beginning, and He'd given them each other to walk through the hard times together. Always remembering, yet always moving forward.

Hayden tugged at the hem of his blue sweater. Maybe he shouldn't have worn it. He was sweating to death.

Elliott, who stood next to him by the Christmas tree, elbowed him in the side. "Knock it off, McGrath. There's no way you're nervous."

"No. Just dying of the heat." Someone had turned on the gas logs, and Mia's living room was blazing hot. Sure, the ambience on Christmas afternoon was great, but it was stifling.

He was definitely not nervous. Marrying Mia on Christmas afternoon was the exact right thing to do.

Was it too fast?

Not at all.

In fact, according to Joann Hale at the Register of Deeds Office, who'd come in on Christmas Eve afternoon to issue their marriage license, they'd taken much longer than anyone had thought they would.

That same sentiment had been echoed by her parents and Noni, who stood by the kitchen door, by his family, who stood beside them, and Pastor Rollins, who stood next to him watching the stairs as they waited for Mia and Ruthie to come down.

Hayden smiled. When they'd told Ruthie that morning that her big Christmas present was going to be her mother marrying her "Uncle Hayden," she'd been so excited that she'd forgotten to open the rest of the packages scattered under the tree. They were still there, wrapped in colorful paper and ribbons. She'd insisted they get dressed immediately, even though their impromptu ceremony wouldn't start until four.

He looked over at Pastor Rollins, who wore jeans and a forest green sweater as he clasped the small three-ring binder that held his notes for the service. "I'm sorry again that we dragged you away from your family's Christmas."

Pastor Rollins snorted. "Dragged me away? They've been waiting for you to marry Mia for a couple of years now. They practically shoved me out the door. Angela even sent me with a wedding present she bought for you guys last year." He gestured to a small gift bag that he'd set on the mantel when he'd walked into the room. "Believe me. The whole town would leave their Christmas dinners behind to be here if you'd invited them."

That might have been a little much, but the sentiment warmed his heart and reinforced the idea that they were doing the right thing. After talking, praying and stealing a few kisses before Ruthie awoke from her Christmas Eye nap, they'd decided not to wait, that a Christmas Day wedding in front of their families in Mia's living room was all they needed.

Everything had fallen into place in a series of answered prayers.

Once they'd talked through everything, they'd known they wanted to spend the rest of their lives with one another starting today, on Christmas. Building new memories of joy on top of the grief that had bonded them.

And they'd certainly received blessings from everyone involved.

His team had jumped into action under Noni's direction to make a huge Christmas dinner to be enjoyed after the ceremony. There was way too much food in the kitchen.

Mia had insisted that she needed no frills, just him.

Ruthie had insisted on dressing them both.

There was no telling what his two favorite ladies would be wearing when they came down the stairs in... He glanced at his watch. Well, right about now.

Sure enough, a rustle near the top step drew everyone's attention.

Ruthie descended, wearing a purple princess dress complete with a tiara. Strapped to her chest was Penelope, decked out in her own tiny pink princess dress.

Hayden choked, but he couldn't decide if it was a laugh or a sob. The precious little girl that he'd loved since the first time she'd grabbed ahold of his finger in her tiny hand was now so much more than his goddaughter. If she ever found out the hold she had over him, she'd be spoiled rotten.

She spotted him and rushed the rest of the way down the stairs, wrapping her arms around his legs and holding on tight. "Mommy's coming, Uncle Hayden, and she's so pretty. And I'm so happy. And so is Penelope."

Forget protocol. He reached down, swooped her up and snuggled her close, planting a kiss on the top of her head. Today could have gone so much differently. When he'd been swimming away from gunfire under swamp water yesterday, he'd never dreamed he'd be standing here just over twenty-four hours later.

There was another sound on the stairs, then Mia descended. She carried the fake flowers that usually sat in a vase on Ruthie's bookcase, a riot of pinks and oranges that the little girl had picked out at the holiday flea market the year before. She wore a pair of jeans and a bright orange T-shirt. A pink scarf was tied around her neck.

Yep, Ruthie had definitely chosen the outfit. It was a riotous blend of her two favorite colors.

Even in the clashing hues that ought to blind everyone in the room, Mia had never looked more beautiful.

When she reached him, she kissed his cheek, then Ruthie's. Threading her arm through his, she laid her head on his shoulder, pulling him tight to her side.

This was it. This was his family. This was where he wanted to be.

He held her close and shut his eyes, taking a moment to thank God for the man who had loved her and had been his best friend from birth, the one whose story had ended too soon.

And then he thanked God for another chapter, a different chapter, one that honored all that had been and all that was yet to come.

* * * * *

Dear Reader,

One of my favorite verses is Psalm 139:16, which talks about God writing down our days in a book even before we were formed. How awesome that He allowed me to put that in a story!

Know why? Because you are special. He cares so much about you that He is protecting your story, providing for you even in the darkest, blackest, most horrible moments. It's comforting to me to know that He saw the ugly coming and made a way through it. I don't have answers for why we suffer on this earth, but I do have complete confidence that God knows, He sees, He hears, He understands, and He makes a way to the other side of it.

How do I know? Because I've experienced it in my own life. I pray you feel His love, too, even in the dark and ugly times. I pray that you feel His presence with you when it all feels hopeless. Believe me, He's there.

This book is also special because I also got to include the Alligator River National Wildlife Refuge. It's one of my favorite places. I had to take a few liberties with the placement of the waterways, but believe me, it is a beautiful, wild, special place where God's beauty is on display. Bonus, it's my "gateway" to the Outer Banks, which is my favorite place of all.

I hope you enjoyed your time with Mia and Hayden (and Ruthie). This is the first book in the Trinity Investigative Team series. Up next, we'll dive into Rebecca's story. To keep up-to-date, visit me at jodiebailey.com! Oh, and Merry Christmas!

Jodie